I0573549

Legend of the Widow Maker

Book Three of the Widow Maker Trilogy

By
Zoez Lajoune

Cadmus Publishing
www.cadmuspublishing.com

Published by Cadmus Publishing
www.cadmuspublishing.com
Port Angeles, WA

ISBN: 978-1-63751-093-3

Also by Zoez Lajoune

The Widow Maker Series

Book 1: The Awakening of the Widow Maker

Book 2: The Rise of the Widow Maker

Book 4: The God Complex

ACKNOWLEDGEMENTS

Warm thanks to all of you who have inspired me to become a griot. To my mother, Brenda Joyce Brown, who has guarded everything I've ever wrote. To my publications liaison, Frank Reuter, at Cadmus Publishing, for patience and incredible support. Last and most importantly, to THE ONE whose grace and mercy lifts me, washes me, and sustains me. You're better to me than this old world could ever be. I write to serve Your purpose and honor.

You first Jesus!

ACKNOWLEDGMENTS

DEDICATION:

I dedicate this book to all of you who will continue to read this compelling story and be changed by it forever.

Disclaimer

This book is a work of fiction. The characters, incidents, and dialog are drawn from the author's imagination and are not to be construed as real. Any resemblance to actual events or persons, living or dead, is entirely coincidental.

Contents

PROLOGUE

For Razee, marriage and life was quite boring, even depressing at times, and he sought to leave. That all changed when he took his Asian princess, Mei Wei, to Wisconsin to meet his extended family. She was normally a quiet girl. One that wore librarian style clothing. That consisted of random themed t-shirts, combat boots and long woolen skirts. Although her eyes sparkled with an oceanic blue that was rare than radium. As a Chinese girl with blue eyes, she felt awkward and never really grasped their beauty. Consequently, she opted out of the LASIK eye surgery and the contact lens that were recommended by her optometrist. Choosing rather to wear a vintage pair of vogue style, coke bottle thick glasses. That hid her eye color well. Her job that was an extension of a Silicon Valley research facility. It required that she stay enmeshed in beakers, petri dishes, and specimen reports. One day, after being convinced by her husband to relax a little at his family reunion. She disappeared into a back bedroom with his crazy, wild-ass cousin from Milwaukee, named Louise. Who was carrying a liter of Wild Irish Rose. 45 minutes later, Mei Wei emerged from the room wearing an unknown camouflage t-shirt. With one of her black pantyhose knee high stockings tied around her left bicep and the other one tied around her forehead like John Rambo. Like a gremlin out of water, Mei Wei, his beautiful Mugwhy, was lost forever. Once she had tasted the forbidden fruit of the poisonous tree. There was no way that she could ever go back to her former life. Very rapidly, an insatiable thirst grew in her. One that demanded her husband find a way at all costs to accommodate her new fashionable lifestyle of partying or adjust to a bland lifestyle at home without her. Once their life savings was depleted and the bills piled up. In drastic times, stupidity led them like many others in choice. To figure out a way to keep the party going, in many well-known strip clubs, bars, and neighborhoods of Minneapolis and St. Paul. Instead of simply adjusting their lifestyle. Knowing that it is best to leave certain things untouched and buried like old bones. Logic gave way to a very foolish, lucrative desire that prompted them. To take up a seemingly easy trade and become a husband-and-wife copycat serial killing team. With a plan to leave behind them a trail of toe tags and orchestrated scenes. Along with the mark of a dark age calling card. That belonged to someone that they believed was derived from old fables, haunted folklore, and obscure myth. That had been cunningly devised to scare uneducated, brainwashed mimes away from seizing the spoils of this life. They thought their plans were bulletproof. With the perfect cloak to lead the authorities on a wild goose chase. To hunt for someone that they claimed five years ago cast the darkest net upon the Twin Cities ever publicized. A cold hand that still help a grip on their souls.

Many had failed to bargain with him. One had foolishly tried to extort him. None had ever tried to steal from him. Especially not out of his own vineyard and claim it as their own. The whisper in the hospital emergency room. The fear too consuming to even utter and intercede against in prayer.

He has returned to protect his legacy and to teach penanced to the unbelieving. That all may show reverence to…

The Legend of the Widow Maker

…myth is not that far from legend.

INTRODUCTION

S ullen eyes that seeped despair and lay under total eclipse of an eternal night stared deep into the darkness of the heavens as thunder rumbled across the sky. The bittersweet nightshade plant of death grew warningly outside of the entryway to her cardboard shelter. The shadow of its leaves hung low and overshadowed the soiled, dingy blue plastic tarp that flapped in the wind and covered the entryway of her door. A magnetic vortex, like a highly volatile dark ether, drew the entire zombified camp like a mindless drove to the doorway of old lady Shelia Parker to hear the final words of the raspy old voice. For evening had come and her heart made preparation to cross over to the other side. She knew that her time had come. That she had cheated death for way too long. Where would her body rest? Although her mind had only begun to relive the nightmares of each brutal and horrific account that she had chronicled and cursedly retold night after night. That anguish would endure until her day for reckoning was at hand. The day when the Lord God would judge the quick and the dead. Secretly in her heart she longed for a cryogenic slumber of sorts. Even if it meant her imprisonment in Tartarus... The dungeons of the Titans that were hunted and caged after they had wrought havoc and destruction upon the Earth. Indeed, that would be a well-deserved box and most appropriate judgement for the Herald of the Light of Death himself... the Widow Maker.

Over the past decade, her health had slowly dwindled. Tragically, she went from being a vibrant, middle aged woman to having a weakened immune system from living for years with the AIDS virus without having the proper antiviral medication. She also developed cervical cancer from multiple delayed treatments of sexually transmitted infections. She had foolishly contracted them during the years she was still an active prostitute of the slain Skinny Pimp. While her high fever, cold sweat, and mucus filled cough caused her to shift longingly for comfort, huge lumps of phlegm slid in her stomach like soft coal as her liver shut down permanently. Suddenly, the flapping of the tarp ceased. The wind didn't blow on the camp anymore, the sound of passing traffic dissipating as the crowd became motionless, quiet and still. The night gave audience to the raspy old voice of Shelia Parker as it burned with each word across her trachea from the bronchitis that had restricted her airway by 40% with mucus and puss.

Some of the women in the camp began to cry as soon as she said, "Only a little while longer am I with you. The Boatman is waiting for me. I can hear the splash of his oars in the water and the rattle of the chains on the deck of the boat as he approaches. Remember all that I have told you. Tell the little ones too. Lest vanity fill their hearts and greed guide them in their decisions just as it has done so many others. Like this foolish, young couple who didn't take the same warning that I am giving to you. They instead made a mockery of the Legend of the Widow Maker and disturbed his slumber. Leaving Carlos no choice except to return from his resting place in the bayous of New Orleans, Louisiana just to collect them."

PART 1: THE TORMENTED SOUL

CHAPTER 1
THE DISCONTENTED HEART

t all began as a thought. A mere whisper in the corner of his mind. A whisper from a voice so foreign, so faint, and so chilling that he could hardly believe it originated in his own heart. The more he tried to ignore it the more it scratched at his mind and posed the rhetorical question, "Is she worth it?" Although he has never asked himself the underlying question as to why her, and was she really worth staying with for life? There was a quietness that life had offered him with her. So, he had taken vows to endure with her through whatever life would bring. Still, his true motive for marrying her really did not have anything to do with her. Rather it was filled with infatuations of suburban life along with an escape from the discords of his former violent life on the east side of Milwaukee, Wisconsin. There was a time in his life when all he thought about was her and she was more than enough. Now after three short years of a life draining marriage, the last two more bitter than the end of the first, he was no longer content, and Mei Wei was not ignorant to that. She noticed how he looked at other women in public. Women that did not appear anything like her. They had sex appeal, wore tight clothing. Garments that complimented their skin, their hair, their eyes, and highlighted the curves of their bodies. They got manicures once a week and pedicures at least twice a month. They carried designer bags, always looked as if they had just walked out of a hair salon and their perfume you could smell long after they had left the room. Mei Wei on the other hand displayed zero sex appeal. She wore baggy clothing that well concealed her petite toned body. She practically bought all her clothing off one rack at Walmart, in addition to the random themed t-shirts that she would buy at record shops and thrift stores strung across the Twin Cities. All of her hair products, cosmetics, and hygiene items came from the local Dollar Tree or CVS Pharmacy. The only fragrance that normally remained in the room long after she left was the lingering aroma of her Subway sandwich, which she buried in banana peppers and ate regularly for lunch. Beneath the odd but technical visage that she portrayed was a stunningly beautiful, blue eyes slightly awkward Chinese girl. She really did not know, like her rare eyes, the rare talents that she possessed.

Huge rain drops tapped heavily against the windows of the hunter green colored 97' Monte Carlo that Ra'zee drove as a work vehicle. Immediately as he and Mei Wei rounded the corner from the CVS Pharmacy and the Ten O'clock liquor store, they noticed that their convenient parking spot in front of their Maplewood home had been taken again. No doubt by someone going to hang out at the city's worst social problem, but who did not want to park in their parking lot due to vandalism and break-ins. The popular Stargate Nightclub sat on the Maplewood side of the three intersecting cities: St. Paul, Maplewood, and Roseville. The club was notoriously known for multiple gang fights, debilitating stabbings, and homicide related shootings. Stargate Nightclub sat about a rock's throw away from their Maplewood home on the opposite side of the railroad tracks. Over time, the club that had once shown promise of increased revenue for other stores developed a scab of unwanted traffic and reoccurring problematic blisters, like a highly infectious mutated form of the shingles virus. Severely impacting the small financial district by driving down sales, many businesses had to close and relocated to safer grounds in the surrounding developing communities.

As they exited, Mei Wei grabbed several thin plastic shopping bags from the backseat of the car. She pinched her jacket closed, tucker her chin in her chest, then turned her head to the left to block the wind and the rain. Ra'zee popped the trunk and moved quickly to grab his weekend nurse aid, a 30 pack of Milwaukee's best beer. As Mei Wei splashed off through several puddles while half blinded by the mix of hard swept wind and rain, Ra'zee called to her, "Hey, wait up." She kept walking until she heard him yell at her half-winded through the rain.

"So, what do you want to do tonight?" He asked hoping that she would want to do more than just stay at home.

She responded through a full yawn, "Ra'zee, I am so tired. I have to be up early to finish detailing the last forensic reports from the specimens our home offices sent last week. We are also expecting a full department review within the next two weeks and our filing system needs to be updated.

Ra'zee asked in frustration, "Why do you have to do everything?".

"If I don't do it then it won't get done. Plus, our department is already understaffed. As a newly appointed manager, it is my responsibility! You knew that when you pushed me to go up for the position." Mei Wei responded irritated.

Ra'zee snapped back, "Hold on, I am not the bad guy here. I only encouraged you to go for it in hopes that it would break you out of your shell more, not neglect me more."

Upon hearing those words, Mei Wei stopped dead in her tracks. He knew how she felt about her job, and he had crossed the line. Angrily she said, "Why do you care about how much I work on the weekends? By morning you will be passed out on the couch with the girl under your arms anyway." Before he could respond, she stomped off through the rain.

Ra'zee pleaded, "Mei Wei, wait. I didn't mean it like that. Don't act like a gremlin my little beautiful Mugwhy."

No answer came except for the harsh slap of the sleet rain against his face. Ra'zee stood there for a moment and listened to the soft pound of the bass from the Stargate Nightclub coming from across the field. The tall grass appeared to sway invitingly under its hypnotic spell. Images of his old extravagant life zig zagged across his mind. "Might as well hit the club since I am paying for it," he mumbled to himself. Then he turned and walked back to the car.

Mei Wei turned around on the bottom step at the house to apologize to Ra'zee for her harsh tongue. With mouth open and a dismissive laugh, she started by saying, "You know honey, I..." Then her voice trailed off into dead silence as she watched the taillights on Ra'zee's car glow red then switch to white as he pulled away. "Figures!" she said angrily in a low voice under her breath. Then she reached in her pocket for her cell phone to call him and ask him to come back. To her surprise, she not only found her cell phone but his as well in another pocket. After that, she remembered that she grabbed it for him when he almost left it in the car at the Ten O'clock liquor store. Her usual thoughts of insecurity furrowed her forehead as she began to speculate how much longer would Ra'zee remain faithful to her or if this would be the night that all things change between him and her.

The club was wall to wall packed. Ra'zee did a quick check over his outfit since it was what he had worn to work. The black jeans, beige Timberland boots, and black/lime green t-shirt that read "Don't rush me, I get paid by the hour!" was good enough. Ra'zee's homeboy named Juvenile was posted with the rest of the security team in the front. When he saw him, he waved him past through everyone else in the line.

Holding his hand to refuse the cover charge money with his ID, Juvenile said, "Oh yeah Raz, that's what you on? Get yourself together. You already know we ain't doing that even though you don't come kick it with your boy no more. Plus, judging by that Walmart ballers outfit that you got on, you probably need those ten dollars more than me. Damn, you still letting your little Asian wife dress you?"

Ra'zee laughed. "What's going down Juvenile? My big dog, damn it's good to see you. Man, its off the chain up in here."

Juvenile smiled as he pointed at Ra'zee and poked him slightly in the chest saying, "You already know what it do up in the Stargate and yo ass can't touch nothing."

"I'm still the man. I can still cuff any broad up in here if I wanted to," Ra'zee said.

Juvenile laughed as he stuttered to say, "Nig.. Nig.. Nigga please. You already know that little Asian woman would come up in here with that Jackie Chan bullshit and beat your ass."

Ra'zee started trying to stunt by reading off his Milwaukee resume, "Boy you know how I get down. That is why my name was ringing hard in the streets when I touched down up here in 2014. Yeah and I..." but Juvenile just smiled and said, "We boys. You ain't got to prove nothing to me. I know you use to be about that life, but that ain't you no more dog. Not even since you took yo ass over in that one Mmong neighborhood over in St. Paul and then married that little Asian girl you met at the record shop. She checked yo ass real quick. First, you quit banging music with her in the car. Then, you disappeared out of the hood and bought that little gingerbread house that you stay in around the corner. Everybody in the hood saying that you got paper fans on the walls in your living room, traded in your pistol for a sword, and she make yo ass eat with chopsticks." Ra'zee fell out laughing as Juvenile bowed to him and said, "I am going to start calling yo ass Cefoo (Chinese for master)."

Out of nowhere Juvenile quit laughing. Ra'zee kept going and said, "I am going to prove to yo big three-hundred-pound, triple whopper eating ass that I still got it and she don't run shit."

Suddenly, Mei Wei yelled at some guy trying to get her number, "I don't want to talk to you, I'm married." Then she pushed past his boy that said, "Man, shortie is fine as hell.. Especially if she take off that cheap ass outfit she wearing. I bet you all that shit came off of the same rack at Walmart."

Mei Wei kept walking as she yelled at Ra'zee with all five feet of her fury. "Ra'zee, I knew that you would be here!"

Ra'zee wiped the smile off his face as Juvenile whispered to him, "It's been nice knowing you dog." Then he said to Mei Wei, "Hey baby girl, good seeing you. Don't worry, I was watching him."

Mei Wei smiled lightly and said, "Hi Juvee, good seeing you." when she hugged him, she practically disappeared into his massive frame.

Juvenile whispered to Ra'zee as he walked past, "If she beat yo ass up in here, I am gonna ban you from the club. We boys, but I can't have you making me look soft in public. I still run the hardest hitting crew in the Twin Cities.

Ra'zee said, "I got this. I'll rap with you in a minute."

Juvenile said, "Get y'all a drink on me. That'll loosen her ass up."

"Good looking out big dog," Ra'zee said. Then he turned toward Mei Wei, who was looking around awkwardly as well as looking awkward. She removed her glasses to wipe the moisture and fog from the lens. It was then that she made eye contact with him and felt her heart melt. For his look said that there beneath the glasses with dripping hair was the only woman that he desired. That he wanted to see more of her and help her to see that none of these ghetto ass broads in the

Stargate could touch her. That in his eyes, she is hands down the baddest bitch in the room. In return, her look told him that she believed in him. That she would be willing to try to change and even follow him to the ends of the earth. If it would keep him satisfied?

Ra'zee smiled and asked, "Do you want to get out of here?"

Reaching for his hand while putting her glasses in her coat pocket, she said shyly, "We can stay for a little while if you like?"

Ra'zee smiled and said, "I am gonna get a drink, you want one?"

Mei Wei giggled and said, "I am fine. I'll sit with you though."

Ra'zee said, "Who knows, you may actually like it here and have a little fun."

Mei Wei looked around at the other girls, how they were dressed and the attention that they were getting by every man in the club. Still unsure of what to think, she said, "It doesn't seem that bad in here." Then, while squeezing his hand even tighter, she said to herself, "As long as you're here to protect me, I will be fine."

At the bar, Ra'zee sipped a double shot of tequila. Mei Wei just watched how it relaxed him as they listened to the music. She could not remember the last time she saw him happy and talking to old friends that had not seen him in a while. Guilt consumed her as she realized that instead of making him happy, she had taken his joy. It was her that had cut him off from life and who was driving him away. That before her was a shadow of the man that she had fallen in love with. Her own stubbornness was turning him into a man that she never vowed to be with, and simply would not find happiness with. It was her who needed to change.

CHAPTER 2
THE CARNIVAL OF CARNAGE

———⊶∘⟨✦⟩∘⊷———

C arlos found himself walking through the Minnesota State Fair grounds at night. There were thousands of people present and laughing underneath the festive lights as he took in the sounds of American Idol auditions and the scents of various appetizing foods. Spread throughout the crowd, there were several dark figures that moved like mist toward him. Each one was wearing a mask that bore a gory image. One mask depicted a sickly clown face that had a large forehead with staples in it, red eyes, and sharp sticky yellow teeth. Another was a live goat's head with what looked like real blood dripping from the fur of its severed collar. Yet another was part hellhound on the left and blank faced mime on the right. Others followed with them that equally bore hellish abstract images. Through it all and past the normal spectators, he couldn't help but notice one broken down concession booth that sat off in the back under a busted flickering light. There was a strange familiarity about that place that he felt drawn to the moment he glanced at it. He tried to look away and take in more of the sights. However, the more he tried to ignore it, the more it scratched at his mind. Feeling compelled beyond reason to venture closer, he weaved through lovestruck couples that shared cotton candy. Parents yelled after their children who ran off in pursuit of toys. To the challenge of "Step right up to try your luck" would be travelers trying to win the prize and concessionaires trying to make a buck. This whole time, he kept an alert eye on the masks that spotted the large number of common people until the crowd thinned out and his view of the abandoned stand became much clearer.

He stopped dead in his tracks upon realizing the abandoned place was indeed the old toolshed from out in the back of his mother's house. Although the front wall had been broken open and converted into a countertop with flaky and peeling, mold covered paint. He was certain that this was it. He soon noticed that there was someone there in the front swinging a heavy, wide head rubber hammer with great violent thrusts. He wore all white from head to toe which consisted of a fedora style brim, wife beater t-shirt, white dress slacks, and hard sole dress shoes. Carlos could tell that he was very muscular, although he didn't pack on a lot of bulk.

As he swung the heavy mallet with intensity to ring the bell of the strong man scale, a dark chuckle would arise from underneath his breath with each malicious swing.

Carlos squinted and stepped to the side to try to see the face of the one before him. Whose face was concealed by the shadow opposite of the flickering light, when the mallet hit the steel plate. A head with no eyes rose swiftly up the scale and rung the rusted bell. With the ring of the bell, Carlos began to hear the familiar chime of six nickels falling to the ground as his vision grew hazy. The Widow Maker turned towards him and grinned through a jawline that was partly covered by decayed flesh. His eyes turned an insidious yellow as he hoarsely said, "Lux Ab Exitium Velle Venere" and held out the bloodied handle of the sledgehammer to him. As Carlos reached for the handle, the Widow Maker yelled fiercely at him, "Wake up young Carlos! That's right my young padawan... wake up."

He was suddenly awakened in the backyard tree hammock by the sound of an old truck. It was coming up the gravel road to Maria's uncles house, down in the bayous. The 1957 Ford pickup was a rusted maroon color. It looked as if it was made of heavy and old, solid steel. Its black tires were so bald that you could see the white thread in them from the porch. A carefully stacked pile of watermelons filled the back. The driver that was stuffed behind the steering wheel had a charcoal black skin complexion from the sun. He wore faded overalls with a dingy white t-shirt that was as yellow as the teeth in his mouth. Slowly he called up to the house from the truck while chewing on a piece of straw that he had in his mouth. His New Orleans was so thick that you had to be from down there to understand a word that came out of his mouth.

"Where Cedric? I say we go pitch a melon. He done burnt a hole in day light enough. You heard me?"

Maria yelled back, "He putting on pants. I'll tell him you said come on."

Carlos just shook his head. For after five years in the bayous, he still didn't understand half the people down there. As he rolled over off the hammock, Maria made her way through the tall grass walking a toddler towards him smiling and said, "I see you finally woke. You hungry?"

Carlos yawned, stretched, and said, "Hey you," oblivious to what she said.

Maria repeated, "You hungry?"

He responded through a yawn shuttered smile, "No beautiful, I am good. I got to get going anyway. I'm supposed to be finishing up rebuilding the front deck porch of the main house at the Stonewall Plantation."

Maria looked surprised as she said, "Old man Stonewall still live in that house?"

Carlos said, "Yeah, him and his caretaker Ms. Hatchfield. Your uncle Cedric cleared the job, although he himself won't go up there."

"I know. They been feuding for over thirty years. Something about some hussie at the juke joint? I guess

Mr. Stonewall lost her to my uncle Cedric?" Maria said.

Carlos laughed and said, "Sounds like she put a fix on both of them?"

Maria replied, "You'd better watch it going up there to that house. Don't mess around and end up like that girl from that movie The Skeleton Key or else old man Stonewall will have himself a new meat suit."

Carlos became possessed by highly vivid thoughts. Staring at the ground he mumbled to himself, "If only they would be so foolish, I wouldn't have to utter the Latin mantra to summon him whose name I dare not speak. For he would come quickly to collect them from tampering with me, his true vessel."

Maria shivered upon hearing those words as her mind was bombarded by a string of odd details connected to Carlos' victims and the manhunt for him in Minnesota. Clippings of newspaper articles detailing the string of murders across the Twin Cities bearing the Widow Maker's calling card blanketed her mind. Those in return triggered the same fear consuming emotions that she had felt the morning she found the two dead bodies stacked in her own bathtub and had relived every time she looked at a bathtub since. Realizing her need for a good distraction right now more than ever she headed over to the gardening patch about fifteen feet away. She took several deep breaths as she squatted and reached for a couple of the tools that had been left behind. Suddenly through the swaying blades of tall grass, she noticed a fresh patch of black soil about eight or nine feet away on her right. It had been cultivated by someone else since yesterday after supper time when she had left the same spot. Her heart told her whatever lay in the soil, she should leave it well enough alone. Ain't no telling what one might find digging in a shallow grave down in the Louisiana bayou.

Curiosity screamed at her that whatever it was, she just had to know. She patted the dirt first and nothing burrowed through. So she slowly eased her fingers beneath the cool surface to feel for the form of what she hoped would put her mind at ease. A puzzled look formed on her face when she discovered that buried in the form of a shallow grave underneath the soil, was a black knapsack. Her throat became bitterly dry as she loosened the draw string and peeked inside. The content of the bag was little soiled cardboard mortuary toe tags each bearing a person's name. Thoughts of dozens of local missing person's news reports (most of which were even too strange for the bayou) all springing up in the last six months. Carlos' recent strange behaviors, fears of something watching her as she soaked in the bathtub at night raced across her mind. Then a vision of a seemingly endless field of highly polished black coffins with a dark figure dressed in all white standing at the end of it appeared in front of her. As the figure began walking toward her, the coffins in his path flipped aside like rapidly falling dominoes. Dropping the small spade in her hand, hiking up her sun dress, and swinging Jaysiah onto her hip, she took off running back up to the house through the field yelling at the top of her lungs.

"Carlos! Carlos!" She wanted to catch him before he left. While she ran, she desperately hoped that the vision had actually been a hallucination of some sort. Not that she had just been infused with some sort of divine tocsin like premonition. That the Widow Maker had indeed returned to collect a payment of souls from a newly found killing field to permanently settle their accounts and balance his eternal ledger. By the time Maria reached the clothing lines on the side of the house, Carlos had already mounted the stack of watermelons in the back of the truck as it was pulling off. As Maria yelled to Carlos and waved at him, he assumed that she was waving goodbye instead of waving him over. Shifting the tool belt on his shoulder, he waved back at her. Maria dropped Jaysiah off her hip and ran out of her flip-flops to the end of the dirt driveway. Winded from her hillside sprint and sweating profusely from the typical 97-degree heat in the bayou, she stopped at the end of the driveway exhausted with both of her hands on her knees and called to him through a low hoarse voice, "Wait... Carlos, I need to tell you something," as if she could telepathically tell him her thoughts. Instead, Carlos continued to wave goodbye as the old, rusted truck rounded the bend in the road that it originally came up. Her thoughts soon began to overwhelm her. Her greatest fear of those caskets being filled with the bodies of people that she personally loved and knew consumed her in an instance.

It had been five long years since she had talked to Carmen McIntyre, Carlos' mom. Out of fear of the police listening to McIntyre's phone calls to discover the whereabouts of her son and whom had been harboring him all this time. So, they agreed to no contact. However drastic times called for drastic measures. She needed Mcintyre's help now more than ever. Especially if it meant that Carlos was in trouble and that the Widow maker's return was eminent. Maria called McIntyre at Regions Hospital in St. Paul, Minnesota, believing that the likelihood of the police taping the phones at the hospital was slim to none due to such a high volume of random phone calls going through the switchboard. When McIntyre answered the phone at the fourth-floor nurse's station, Maria wouldn't waste no time with polite pleasantries or talk of should a, would a, could a regrets. For she knew that Carlos' mom understood everything about her son and that he had gone to see her before they left. However, she did not know that the Widow Maker had spoken to McIntyre separately about Carlos and their return one day.

McIntyre had just excused her current training class to go to an early lunch while she sat and laughed with Misty, an ER nurse. When she answered the phone, a lighthearted laugh was still on her breath. "Good afternoon, fourth floor nurses' station. This is RNT McIntyre. How may I help you?"

Talking fast, in fragmented thoughts and not making

much sense while telling the day's events: Carlos' words about being the true vessel, the bag of toe tags buried in a shallow grave of fresh dirt, and the vision of the field of coffins. She bounced around from three different parts. Maria didn't even take time to tell McIntyre who she was. McIntyre told Maria to take a deep breath. Misty walked away to go finish up some paperwork, thinking that McIntyre was just on another call to help a patient panicking over something that was not as serious as they initially believed that it was.

CHAPTER 3
PROSPECTS OF THERAPY

D r. Rutowski was met by his personal assistant at the isolation wing of St. Peters psychiatric hospital ward and then escorted through the security checkpoints and into a conference room. There they sat as his patient was wheeled in, secured to a standing restraint bed like Dr. Hannibal Lector from the move Silence of the Lamb.

"Good morning Dr. Rutowski. How are you doing today?" she asked through the spit bag that covered her head.

"I am well and how are you?" he responded. No verbal response was offered this time. Only innocent eyes underscored by a mischievous smile.

Nevaeh Sharai smiled as Dr. Rutowski gave her the cue to debrief him on the status of the patient in front of him. While he played the video footage given to him by the onsite staff, she stated the obvious, "I am sure you are aware of the recent developments that unfolded here yesterday morning."

Dr. Rutowski cut back in, "what exactly happened again?"

Nevaeh took a deep breath. Then she said, "Well for the most part, it had been quiet and tranquil for most of the staff and patients the entire morning here at St. Peter Psychiatric Hospital. However, that abruptly ended shortly after Louise Middleton here experienced a travesty at her release hearing in court." Louise waved a pinky finger at them from her cross armed restraint vest. While Dr. Rutowski reviewed the tape, Nevaeh finished narrating the account and said, "She became overwhelmingly angry about the judge extending her time here. Staff informed me that upon her return, she appeared visually irritated and started complaining about her clothing, threatening to call the government and bouncing off of the walls. Staff issued warnings to her several times through the plexiglass window of the security bubble. She was told by one of the staff members to settle down and to not push it, as it was not going to end the way she was thinking. Another staff member's account went farther as she informed me that in a stare-down that was the equivalent of a five-year old's response to their mother's challenge to take off their favorite dirty t-shirt and to take a bath, that Louise shot a testing smile at each one of them.

Quickly, the guard monitoring the day room smiled invitingly right back at her. Then he patted the leather case, on the counter next to him. That contained the two injection vials of the highly effective tranquilizer, Chlorpromazine.

The guards trump card was soon met by Ms. Middleton here spinning around, pulling down her pants and planting her butt firmly on the security bubble's plexiglass. Immediately her undignified, unchaste behavior sent the other patients into an uproar. Some yelled at the psychiatric aids about cartoon movies. Some protested by slinging mashed potatoes and mixed vegetables against the plexiglass window. One elderly man stripped naked, lifted his walker above his head, and proceeded to shout, "Our liberation is at hand! Follow me people!" Then, as several of the aids rushed in to get control of the room, a couple of patients that were only there pretending to be in dire need of psychiatric care to try to convince a doctor to sign off on them receiving SSI benefits. They went and stood in the corner for to them, because this was a level of madness that not even they were quite ready to succumb to.

Oddly, only one person remained sitting, smack dead in the center of it all. Patient number 525-7600, Lavelle. He is known for normally being peaceful but is also known for spontaneous and wild outbursts of anger that are often proceeded by strange and unusual smells of snack food. There he sat quietly in the midst of the chaos, as though in his mind all of the yelling taking place was like one of Beethoven's romantic musical compositions.

Meanwhile, Louise, which still held her butt against the floor to ceiling plexiglass barrier, kicked into third gear as she danced back and forth. All the while, according to several patients that volunteered statements, that she was making a squeaky noise with her butt against the window. Three of the staff members intervened and wrestled Louise to get her under control. While they pinned her against the glass, she tried to wiggle free as she yelled, and I quote..." Nevaeh looked down and read the statement off of the official report. ""' I know you stole my money. I was going to order some chicken with that money. Now you going to try to make me sit down. You are no match for the great and powerful Lou-I-s-e!" end quote. Well, while the words were still leaving her mouth, the hypodermic needle was entering her left buttock muscle. In one long and slow streak, her bare butt slid down the glass.

Then, like a fish out of water, Louise lay there with her eyes in the top of her head and drooled. Suddenly, her alleged in house boyfriend, Lavelle, stood up and yelled, "Hey Louise! I. Smell. POPCORN" Louise lifted a limp arm off of the floor and swung one finger in the direction of her attackers. Then through a slurred voice, like a disoriented commander in chief, she told him, and I quote..." Nevaeh looked down and read again. "" Thats right honey, you get em'.""" end quote. Nevaeh closed the file in front of her just as Lavelle plowed his way through another patient plus two guards and covered himself in three trays of mashed potatoes, mixed vegetables, and gravy that were still on the table. The video footage froze and the phrase 'resume play' blinked in the upper left-hand corner of the screen.

Dr. Rutowski quickly set the remote control down on the table and momentarily glanced at Ms. Middleton. A smile slowly formed on his face as he folded his arms across his chest, closed his eyes, removed his glasses, and stroked the bridge of his nose. This unconscious habit of his reluctantly showed his high levels of stress.

"You can't be serious?" He stated rhetorically. "You were doing so well Louise. What happened to you using your de-escalation steps from group after your red flag cues of H-hungry, A-angry, L-lonely, T-tired surfaced?" He opened his eyes and looked at her with a warm look of concern as he left his chair and made his way across the room. He sat down on the edge of the table in front of her and then asked, "Were you having trouble thinking clearly again?"

At first, she tried going off on a tangent of mixed singing and pouting from her upright restraint board position just a few feet away from the end of the long, polished cherry oakwood table. When that discourse ran dry, Louise looked at him with doe-like eyes and spoke with a child-like voice through the spit bag as if she honestly believed that she was innocent in all of this. Halfway through hearing the plight of Louise Middleton, in that she had been led in this tandem of unruly behavior unwillingly by an alien entity who forcibly impregnated her through a digitized phone call by the US government. And that this was an extraterrestrial conspiracy to bring our two species together, and that as a cipher she simply could not control the actions of the other being until her body adapted to its DNA. She went on to say that if someone would just let her call her contact with the Secret Service, that they would verify everything. Her voice faded in his hearing her story, as Dr. Rutowski lost his equilibrium and felt his soul recoil within himself. Huge salt-colored beads of sweat permeated the skin of his forehead, and his mouth became dry like the Wilderness of the Sin. He cringed as his body temperature spiked sharply, like a soprano's acapella note.

Having witnessed Dr. Rutowski go through this Dr. Jekyll fade into Mr. Hyde type of transformation multiple times in mid dialogue over the past five years. She knew well what would soon follow these physical signs but did not know what physical threat she would face. Just in case she needed to quickly remove herself from the room, Nevaeh Sharai instinctively and slowly repositioned her chair towards the door as Dr. Rutowski gripped the edge of the table to steady himself. Cosmic flashes of light shot through his eyes as he began to hear the familiar chime of six nickels falling to the ground as his vision grew hazy.

The Widow Maker interjected with a dry, hoarse voice, "Tsk, tsk, tsk. Ms. Middleton, whatever shall we do with you?" While my counterpart believes in mercy, I believe in penance. The time has come for us to pursue an axiom of alternative medicine that would explore the possibilities for success as well as the potential ramifications of failure by introducing electroconvulsive therapy into this equation. While in many circles, it is held to be cruel, even barbaric, and very controversial by many of my own colleagues. I personally believe that this widely, misunderstood field of therapy was abandoned too early while still being a diamond in the rough. For like all prodigies, though neglected, their potential can never truly be buried. Since the mind is a terrible thing to waste, I say that we waste no more time. That pin there on the side of your restraint board can easily be released to change the vertical position of the board to a horizontal examination table. That would serve my purpose perfectly." A sadistic smile formed on his face as he continued, "Now, don't worry there Ms. Middleton. This procedure should go by nicely. I say that your chances for success are in the high teen percentile. Good enough odds for any doctor." Quickly, he looked down at the floor for a brief moment and further stated, "Look at it this way Ms. Middleton. After this session, you'll be totally cured." Then making eye contact with her once again, he underscored his last statement of certainty in her change with, "regardless of the outcome."

Nevaeh Sharai gasped at the thought of witnessing such a torturous act. Those thoughts intensified immediately when he pulled a highly polished nickel from his pocket and began to roll it down the miniature staircase of his knuckles over and over again in silence. Then, viscously he smacked the table with the palm of his hand and yelled urgently over his shoulder to her and requested, "Ms. Sharai, go fetch me an extension cord and two wet towels. Also bring a spoon or something to wedge in Ms. Middleton's mouth so that she doesn't choke on her own tongue."

He paused and winked at Louise who was wide eyes on the restraint board. Then he continued to say, "Do see if you can find me a small garbage can or pail. Patients have been known to vomit from time to time as well as defecate on themselves in between attempts to reset the brain. I personally think that the whole letting loose of one's bowels helps the patient to relax more, so that they may receive the full benefits of the treatment." He winked at Louise again.

In an attempt to save Louise, Nevaeh Sharai said, "Um, Dr. Rutowski, maybe this procedure, although thoughtful, is a bit hasty? Due to Ms. Middleton having a minor emotional setback after being denied release in court, a setback she can assure you will not happen again in the future."

The Widow Maker looked at Louise who nodded her head rapidly in agreement, then warmly stated, "Perhaps we can reschedule this session to a later date? So that Ms. Middleton here can have adequate time to adjust to her newly acquired skill set. However, if all measures fail, I will make room in my schedule to accommodate you." A warm puddle of urine began to form under the wheels of the restraint board as Louise pissed on herself at the thought of her next session with Dr. Rutowski.

Nevaeh asked, "Shall we be going now?"

The Widow Maker waved at Louise with a pinky finger as he smiled and said in a low voice, "Until next time my dear, and just remember." Then he slowly sang the words under his breath, "He's making a list and checking it twice. He's gonna find out who's naughty or nice." One of his eyes held its gaze on her through the cracked door until it closed.

In the hall, an attendant asked, "How did it go?"

The Widow Maker stated over his shoulder as he walked off, "I believe Ms. Middleton has experienced a major breakthrough and has finally let go of all that was holding her back." Then, turning to Nevaeh, he asked coldly, "Who is next on my list?"

CHAPTER 4
STONEWALL PLANTATION

While the words that testified of the dark intent of his heart fell steadily from his tongue, the Widow Maker heard the brief chant of the Latin inscription "Lux Ab Exitium Velle Venure, Lux Ab Exitium Velle Venere" being used as a summoning prayer resound louder and louder in his ears. Like a bumble bee dangerously drinking nectar from a Venus Flytrap, Nevaeh Sharai instantly noticed when the venom of his words stopped flowing. Unlike any time before his lexicon became disheveled with the impediment of a thousand tongues, the Dark One stopped abruptly in the center of the hall. Light receded from his eyes like the winter sun upon a frozen lake in transition from dawn to dusk. An epileptic shudder grabbed hold of him as he braced the wall for balance.

Then, a vacuum with the force of a black hole created a vortex that caught the tail of his spirit like a comet and literally tore him from the vessel of Dr. Rutowski's body. When he came through the other side, he found himself standing in front of Carlos, who sat cross legged in the tall unkept grass, by a sediment filled pond on the backside of Stonewall Plantation.

As the Light of Death stood upon the murky waters, the sky turned a mix of dark green with lime- colored electrical pockets that sparked within several clouds. A boisterous wind blew like a whirlwind all around him. Slowly, he lifted his head and glanced at Carlos from beneath the fedora style brim. His eyes glowed with subtle enticement for blood as he seethed through a jawline partly covered by decayed flesh, "Why have you summoned me? Do you have a worthy offering for me?"

Carlos no longer felt the cold, but familiar student to teacher bond that he had grown accustomed to. Now he only felt a client to contract killer vibe about this encounter. The Widow Maker walked across the waters as if on solid ground until the soles of his shoes rested on the shore of the pond.

He asked again, "Why is it that you have summoned me?" Carlos said nothing as he stood and looked over his shoulder toward the Stonewall mansion. Stonewall Plantation had acquired many obscure legends since its foundation was laid 125 years ago. Legends like in the beginning it was a chosen nesting ground by many unwanted things that had hid abroad the slave ships, which travelled from the horn of Africa to the New World. In particular, it was the original feeding ground for the Desmodontidae nocturnal: the vampire, the undead. The house was a soiled, decrepit ashen gray. Thick streaks of oil seeped out of the foundation stones that lined the base of the house. That made it eerily looking as if the house itself was shedding the blood it had collected over the last thirteen decades. There was a small family burial plot that marked the front of the house opposite the shade of an old dry bramble bush. Several Confederate markings were etched into the remains of the old broken headstones. A rocking chair on the front porch creaked as if an unseen soul was sitting in it, guarding the entrance to the house.

Carlos pointed towards the house, and the Widow Maker made his way through the field. Carlos watched for a brief moment from a distance, then quickly followed behind him. Just as they emerged from the tall grass, Ms. Hatchfield wheeled old man Stonewall outside onto the front porch for some fresh air. Craftily, she spoke while adjusting the blanket on his lap, "There's a storm coming soon, rather early tonight. Do you think you'll be finished with the deck porch by then?"

Carlos looked at the sky then at the Dark One and said, "I sure hope so. It would be bad if I were to get stranded here."

Ms. Hatchfield continued as she brushed food crumbs off old man Stonewall's shirt, "You're more than welcome to use anyone of the guest rooms if need be. I only ask that you stay out of the attic."

Carlos looked at the ground and wondered what was in the attic. This was probably the fifth or sixth time she had mentioned it being off limits in the month he had worked there. He had never tried to go in there before, so why did she keep bringing it up? It's almost as if she wanted him to grow curious and go in there. Old man Stonewall's hand began to shake as he attempted to lift his finger to point. It had been years since he suffered from the stroke that paralyzed him from speaking. Days, often weeks, would go by that he wouldn't even try. He'd spent his entire life in the bayous and hadn't left Stonewall Plantation one time in the last thirty years. No, not after being confined to his wheelchair of which he also slept in. It is said that over the years, the lost souls in that house used his body as a host. Each one taking turns to share the light in his body to live again for a few hours in one day. The souls of tortured slaves, cruel task masters, run away teens, gullible mistresses, and naïve would-be caretakes had become connected to his soul and given him an extrasensory perceptibility. He could see beyond the natural veil and into the spirit realm.

As if a seizure was about to take him again, he began to moan in fear as he rang the help bell on his wheelchair and beheld the Light of Death standing a couple feet back from the side of Carlos. Repeatedly, he called, "Mmm, mmm.. Ring.. Ring..ring... Mmm, mmm" until

Ms. Hatchfield looked down at him. Suddenly, a gust of wind blew heavily against the house. The Widow Maker climbed the steps and his weight rattled one of the loose boards of the porch and slid it out of its place. While it fell from the porch, Ms. Hatchfield looked down at the sound and said, "My, the wind is getting strong. I reckon that's what's got him so wound up. I'd better take him back inside."

The wind snatched open the screen door just as she turned the wheelchair and the Widow Maker walked into the house. Old man Stonewall fussed and groaned all the more as Ms. Hatchfield pushed him inside right behind the Dark One. Carlos smiled mischievously and said, "It appears that the new master of the house has come home."

Ms. Hatchfield yelled from inside the house in a curious voice, "You know Carlos, I can't quite seem to put my finger on it, but something seems awfully different about you today, almost hungry wolf like. Is there something on your mind?"

In his mind's eye, Carlos witnessed himself chisel the ancient seal of Egyptian Blackness, the dark side of his soul, Animus, on the two front pillars of the house. Although it was his young, boyish hand that held the spike, it was the weathered tattered hand of the Widow Maker that struck it with the grime covered hammer. A dim motion light glossed over each of his eyes like a passing flame from a candle in a mirror. Instantly, he became magnetized to a sequence of augury thoughts about Ms. Hatchfield losing her mind in the house. He watched as she appeared to be under a sleepwalker trance when she came out of the house on a cold and wet, sun smitten day. She dragged a heavy tractor hitch rope in one hand. All of the souls that she had witnessed being tortured over the years gathered one by one from the field on the front lawn adjacent a harvest of dying corn. She tossed one end of the heavy rope through an opening in the old cast iron mold that hung from the face of the house which read, "Stonewall Cotton". Those gathered in the front rose slowly to their feet from sitting in chairs. He watched as she tightened the noose around her neck, climbed the unsteady rocker, and hung herself between the two pillars from the sign. Her feet twitched as she slightly swung and twirled back and forth until the sheer weight of her body snapped her neck.

Just as one shoe slipped from her foot, he noticed the edge of one of the wheels from old man Stonewall's wheelchair protruding through the dirt bed in the old family burial plot. Faintly, he could hear the old man's muffled cries coming through the worm-infested soil. The sound of the thunderstorms building in the distant sky rumbled to give warning of their impeding presence. Then, the sound of lightning striking cracked, only no light flashed. Instead, there was a dark silhouette of the Widow Maker that flickered across the porch from the light coming from the entryway of the door to the house telling of his actual presence. Suddenly, the vision was gone, and Carlos responded to her, "Now that you've mentioned it, I do feel quite hungry."

Upon entering the house, a very rank odor snatched the pleasant countryside air right out of his mouth. Instantly, he remembered why he never ate anything there that he couldn't personally open out of a sealed store snack bag. The dining room table was covered with a heavy old hard plastic sunflower decorated cloth. It had multiple cigarettes burns in it and smelled as if it had been wiped off with a mildew rag that was soaked in ten-day old cabin water. The dishes were half washed, showing dried food and gravy on them. A flower vase filled with what appeared to be dirty water, dead plant leaves, and weeds adorned the table. Only two places were set at the table, one for Mr. Stonewall and one for Ms. Hatchfield. Unlike times before when the house would be quiet, Carlos could faintly hear the crackling sound of an old radio station playing spiritual music, "when we've been there ten thousand years..." whispered through the halls. His mind immediately recalled the sternness in Ms. Hatchfield's voice about the attic being off limits. Even though he had already figured out by now that she really wanted him to go up there. He was beginning to question why. Then he said, "To hell with her. So, what if I take a quick look?"

While Ms. Hatchfield made herself busy in the kitchen, old man Stonewall sat parked in his wheelchair facing the grandfather clock, on the side of the staircase leading to the upstairs. Ms. Hatchfield had been his personal caretaker for the last fifteen years. For the most part, she looked well after him. She made effort to talk to him on the regular. Often he sat there in his chair and never looked at her or even made an attempt to say anything back. Sometimes, she would take him in the bathroom with her when she took a bath. Something had to still be alive in him, because whenever he saw her fat three chin, double stomach, 44 double D naked body sitting in that shallow bathwater, since she was too big for the tub and her body mass would only allow a little water in it. He would lift his shaking hand to try to move the soap suds off her huge breasts. If she turned him toward the window so that he couldn't see her, he would moan and fuss all the time she was in the tub to try to get her attention and hopefully a better view. The grandfather clock appeared to have the same effect on him as the spinning fixture above a newborn babies' crib. Carlos interrupted Stonewall's child-like fascination when he came and stood over his shoulder.

"How's it going today Mr. Stonewall? You feeling better?" He asked as he placed a hand on his shoulder. Old man Stonewall looked down at the hand on his shoulder and went into a downright fit. The muscular hand with contorted fingers of the Widow Maker exposed several knuckles down to bone stripped of half of its skin. One of his fingernails was missing. Dirt and grime packed the rest of them. Too fearful to look over his shoulder and into the eyes of the Light of Death himself, he began to fuss and moan as loud as he could.

Ms. Hatchfield came in from the kitchen. "What are you fussing about now?" she asked.

Upon hearing the sound of glass hitting the floor and shattering into a million pieces, Carlos quickly turned and asked, "Is everything okay?"

Ms. Hatchfield said nothing as she looked at Carlos standing over Mr. Stonewall, then at the corresponding reflection of the Widow Maker standing over Mr. Stonewall, through the glass door of the grandfather clock in his place. Ms. Hatchfield shook her head and dismissed the image as a hallucination. Meanwhile, the Widow Maker crossed over into their realm from the reflective side of the clock and headed upstairs to the attic.

CHAPTER 5
THE CORRUPT PRINCESS

R a'zee woke up just as the sun started to set on the horizon behind his Maplewood home. Mei Wei lay quiet, totally naked in bed with only a sheet wrapped around her waist. Passion flooded his mind as he watched her skin glow under the fiery glare of the sun light. Although she was as boring as a Tuesday night jigsaw puzzle at times, right now she looked like a Christmas morning with that silk sheet tied around her waist like a bow. He couldn't resist the urge to lean in and smell her natural body scent, which was like warm, pecan cookies right out of the oven. Sitting up in bed, he lit a Newport and allowed his thoughts to drift. His eyes traced the tips of her toes and the heels of her small, delicate feet.

He recalled how lost she looked last night in the club

surrounded by the crowd arrested by the bass of the beat. Her appearance was the equivalent of a domestic house cat in the wild out of its natural habitat. The other animals sensed that she didn't belong there. The eyes of something primal were watching over her. Like a baby tasting candy for the first time, curiosity flashed in her eyes at all that she heard and saw in the concrete jungle. Her body language showed a great deal of tension at first, with her mind red hot from anticipation and on high alert to fend off a beast that may spiring forth to ambush her and her husband. Gradually though her fears subsided, her pulse dropped, and her nerves eased. For she realized that although danger is real, her fears were quite foolish. Several nods of the head and whispers of the nickname "Decimal" toward Ra'zee reminded her that she was with a true alpha among common street beasts. He was the most deadliest predator this side of the jungle and everyone there knew that.

Both his name and reputation were not just something that he used to be in one of the hardest hitting projects of Milwaukee, Wisconsin called Hillside. He had also put in a lot of work proving that title in Minnesota too. The name Decimal sent a very clear message that first and foremost, he only got involved with major money moves in the streets. Secondly, that if drama was necessary, he had no problem with sliding on anyone and getting straight to the point. He had so seared his legacy like a hot, branding iron upon the minds of many so-called contenders in St. Paul's Frog Town and across south Minneapolis that even a string of neighboring cities that many thought were safe havens from drama also proved to be false against him. For anyone who harbored someone that had tried to short him, had drama with him or tested the limits of his resolve. They quickly found out how savage he was and equally shared the same fate if they didn't get the hell out of his way. It quickly got to a point in his establishment that he had no qualms with shooting someone in a public place full of witnesses. He often crossed the line in that he took the drama where many wouldn't go.

Like the time he beat the hell out of a guy named Magic at his 82-year-old grandmother's house on her birthday, which to many in the streets was equal to hallowed ground at a church. Magic had ducked Decimal for two months on a $5,000 payment. He owed him for security info to some pawn shop that sat off 10th Curry in downtown Minneapolis. When Magic lost the security blueprint in a high stakes dice game of which Decimal had paid good money for and set up as a jewelry heist, it was on. The money payment was an extension of Decimal's grace to keep him off his ass. Someone who wanted to score points with Decimal caught wind of Magic hiding at his grandmother's house. To prove their loyalty, they not only told Decimal her address, but they also went with him to execute his signature move on his harbored prize. That consisted of stripping him naked, hog tying him, tossing him in the trunk of a stolen car full of rats, and driving him around for hours while he went on to collect other debts.

In Decimal's mind, class was always in session and there were always life lessons to teach. For what he knew that many failed to understand was that there is a difference between the classroom and life. That difference is purely that in the classroom, you're taught a lesson then given a test. However, in life, you are given a test that often teaches a lesson. Decimal did his damn best to underscore both types of lessons at the same time whenever the opportunity presented itself. Unfortunately, for many this double-edged sword would serve as a painful epitaph upon one headstone. Commemorating a costly set of foolish choices in one life, then as a warning to all others of which stated, "Here lay the fool that tried to cheat Decimal. In the end he found his proper place in this box and there's a vacancy right next to him."

Mei Wei yawned lightly then grunted long and hard in protest to Ra'zee shaking her leg to get up.

"No, come back to bed with me," she pleaded.

Ra'zee said, "I would love to beautiful, but we are already running late. We have got six and a half, maybe seven hours on the highway to get to Milwaukee. It's already six o'clock and I really want to touch down by eleven o' clock, so that I can go shoot some pool with a couple of my guys."

Mei Wei slowly started to remember being with him at the club last night. Yeah, she felt awkward and out of her comfort zone, like it was kind of silly being there and wasn't quite sure that she wanted to go back with him. But then she thought about what it had meant to Ra'zee and how alive he looked now. He looked like he was finally awake after a long winter's nap. She could tell by looking at him and listening to him that something had changed in him. He was very agile when he moved, comfortable with each step, almost cat-like. She was sure that he had found himself last night and was somehow more attractive because of it. That's why she fell in love with him in the first place. He was confident of who he was, what he wanted, and how to get it. At least that's exactly how he approached her. She was mesmerized by the fact that he could have just about any woman in the city and all he seemed to want was her. They both knew that on the spectrum of lifestyles, they were polar opposites.

Secretly in her heart, she knew that from the first time he walked in her job at the Cheapo Discount Record shop at 1300 Lake Street in downtown Minneapolis, that she would have a very difficult time telling him no if he asked her to do anything. For some reason as her coworker giggled, shook her arm and said, "Look what just walked in the door." She noticed all kinds of things about him as her friend's daydream grew elusive to her hearing. Like how his smile appeared to be both dominant and yet subtly seductive. She also could tell that he was used to being the center of attention although it wasn't something that he coveted.

The moment he noticed her standing on the side of

her star-struck friend, something grabbed a hold of him as he looked past the long blue jean skirt, combat boots, and coke bottle thick glasses that she was wearing. As if the Divine hand of Christ had personally thrown him a lifeline to escape the chaos of his daily life, he instantly became magnetized to her soul. Complete soberness washed over him, and he knew right then that she was the only music he had truly come in that store for, had waited a lifetime for. That the compilation of all of his conquests had led him to her and that he couldn't leave this store without her. It is believed by many that attraction is purely animal. Nothing more than a chemical secretion of pheromones and decoded body language decrypted by the mind that influences the behavior of others of the same species. This belief, however primal as is or may seem, bear a lot of truth. Still, Chinese philosopher Confucious once said that "The gem cannot be polished without friction nor man perfected without trial." Every trail he had passed, every disadvantage he had overcome, and every obstacle he had defeated. All the friction of his life that he had pressed through had brought him to this moment. It had well prepared his heart to appreciate the gift of God that she was. For to him, she was perfection.

Boldly, he moved towards her slowly, lifting his hands to remove her glasses. She didn't blink as her eyes widened to reveal the rarity of her bright oceanic blue eyes. "There you are. I am Ra'zee, and what do I call you?" he said as he placed her glasses on top of her long, shiny jet-black hair.

Nervously, she stuttered in a beautiful Green Hmong accent, "Um, my name is either Mei or Wei. I mean Mei Wei."

Knowing her culture well, he asked, "Do you know of a nice quiet spot where I can get a really good cup of tea?"

Mei Wei smiled shyly and as she was getting ready to speak, her coworker aggressively stepped between her and Ra'zee and said, "There's a Caribou coffee shop not too far from here that has really good tea."

Ra'zee stepped back and said, "Thanks for the suggestion, but I was hoping for something a little more traditional."

Mei Wei pushed her out of the way and asked her rhetorically, "Don't you hear those three customers at the checkout counter? Plus, don't you have to get home to your five kids?" The other girl rolled her eyes and walked off as Mei Wei put her glasses back on and looked at Ra'zee with gritted teeth.

Ra'zee smiled and laughed slightly as he said, "Beauty and aggression, I think I will call you Mugwhy."

Mei Wei laughed and said, "Me? I am not aggressive, it's her. She brings the gremlin out of me."

Ra'zee asked, "So will you have tea with me?" I'd love to finish this conversation, but my car is running, and I am parked damn near on the bus stop."

Mei Wei laughed and said, "I thought you said you wanted directions for tea? I don't have teatime now; I have to work. Plus, I don't even know you. You could be psycho for all I know."

Ra'zee laughed even harder and said, "Listen, I am no good with directions. You wouldn't want me to get lost and end up with supermarket tea, now, would you? I promise you; I am not psycho. You can trust me, I am an anger management counselor."

Mei Wei started laughing even harder. After about a minute or two, she looked him in the eyes over the top of her glasses and asked, "Only tea?"

He straightened right up like a choir boy and raised his right hand like he was about to swear on the Bible in court. He quickly responded, "Only tea."

She said, "I can pick the place."

He said, "Your choice."

She said, "I get off at 3pm, meet me at..." but before she could finish, Ra'zee quickly interjected.

"I'll be back at five minutes to 3", and he turned to leave.

"I didn't tell you where to meet me," Mei Wei exclaimed.

"It'll be easier if we go together," he said.

"Who said I was getting in your car?"

He said, "I also figured whatever place you chose is close by. We can walk together if that's okay with you or I could stay and follow you there?"

She said, "fine, fine okay, we will walk together. Just leave before you get me fired."

Ra'zee asked, "Would it make you mad if you got

fired for talking to your anger management counselor?" Mei Wei laughed, stomped both of her feet, turned her head, and pointed to the door.

"Go before I change my mind Ra'zee."

He smiled as he left the store and in a teasing voice, he said, "See you later my little Mugwhy."

Mei Wei shook her head and smiled as she headed towards the backroom and said under her breath, "He could have at least bought something. I wonder what kind of music does he even like?"

Back at home, Mei Wei turned over in bed and shuttered with a long, rigid, pointed toe stretching yawn. Then, she grabbed Ra'zee's clean shower t-shirt and pulled it on to go pee. When he noticed his shirt missing, after that he put out his cigarette and grabbed his boxers.

He yelled grumpily after her, "Why do you always do that?" No response came as he reached the bathroom and found her in the shower.

Smiling, she said, "What took you so long Decimal?"

Excitedly, he said, "My little Mugwhy!"

CHAPTER 6
THE FRUIT OF THE POISONOUS TREE

I-94 was overly congested by the time that Ra'zee and Mei Wei had finished their shower together and actually left the house. The Minnesota Viking's football game had generated a lot of traffic clear across the Twin Cities. The excitement was centered around the impressive winning streak that they had built. The result was the chance of becoming the first NFL football team in history to hometown host and play in the Superbowl. By the time the highway traffic had cleared, they were in Eau Clair, Wisconsin.

Ra'zee's mom, Alvona, had already amassed a house full of people that anticipated his return. It had been damn near a year since he had been back in Milwaukee. In that time, many things had drastically changed.

Ra'zee's absentee father, Jesse, had shown up in his usual two-year cycle. Only this time, he came with terminal cancer. The pulmonary specialist's prognosis of a rare type of carcinomatosis proved to be all too accurate. It described what many knew had been coming for a long time, for no one could live the type of life that Jesse had lived and not end up with piss poor health. There were so many ulcerous, golf ball sized tumors that had metastasized all over his body that they were visible on the bottom of his feet, his groin area, and his face. The result of years of being a connoisseur of high-grade marijuana along with a nasty habit of Skull Vodka had been long anticipated and overall left his skin with the thin bubbling discoloration of being injected with battery acid. Ra'zee didn't really look forward to seeing him. Too many painful memories existed between them. Memories of his mom wearing sunglasses from Jesse putting his hands on her. Memories of the public embarrassment he felt as his dad drove by in his nice car, while him and his mom bummed transfers to get on the bus or walked home from the food shelf with other neighborhood kids. However bitter his memories were, nothing pissed him off more than the realization that through it all, his momma remained faithful to Jesse. She had loved Jesse then and still did to this day.

The highway curve going through downtown Milwaukee toward Chicago was lit up brightly. The array of skyscrapers sitting off Lake Michigan had sleek new architectural designs from renovations. If there was one thing that the city of Milwaukee was good at, it was putting a facelift on existing buildings. Ra'zee thought about where he grew up at in Hillside Apartments and how it got smaller every time he saw it. No doubt, it was part of the cities two-part plan. First, to relocate low-income families to the suburbs and convert the ghetto-like neighboring Lapam Park into high priced condos. Secondly, to market the remodeled downtown area as a tourist attraction. Ra'zee just knew that Hillside, with all its legacy, would eventually fall on the permanent conversion list. That night, when the headlights on Ra'zee's car shone through the window at his momma's house, she was the only one that noticed.

"Hey, my only son," said a warm, playful voice backed by a smile that was like warm cotton candy. Mei Wei laughed as she watched him turn into a five-year-old kid being greeted by his mother after his first day at school. She eased out of the car and grabbed her overnight bag from the backseat. Then, she heard, "Mei Wei, you'd better get over here and give me a damn hug girl. Oh my, look at that long pretty hair you've got! I should take your cute little ass over to the hair shop and get paid!"

Just like Ra'zee, Mei Wei's face lit up as the closest woman to a mother she had known in years called her name in roll call as if she had come out of her very own womb. Mei Wei hadn't spoken to her mother in years. When she decided to date Ra'zee, it created a lot of tension. Her parents downplayed the whole arrangement to the rest of their family as a fad she was going through, like her many weird clothing styles. Soon after they dismissed it, the real shocker came as she announced that her and Ra'zee planned to marry. Her parents traditional Hmong views could bear no more. Leaving them with no choice but to completely cut her off. Mei Wei hadn't spoken to her mother in almost four years. Hearing Alvona's voice in how she called to her, fussed over, and accepted her always warmed her heart.

"Ma, I missed you so much. I couldn't wait to see you," she said as she smiled adoringly and reached for Alvona's hand.

"Honey, what are you doing outside in this weather?" said Alvona's older brother, Uncle Frank, as he stepped outside onto the porch. "Hey nephew! Boy, it's good to see you again. I see you got that pretty little wife of yours with you." Ra'zee smiled and Mei Wei blushed. "Girl you look good. You know you remind me of my first wife?"

Uncle Frank had been married three times and was working on a hot, little 29-year-old from the Philippines named Jenny. Whenever Mei Wei came down to visit, Jenny, and Ra'zee's crazy ass cousin named Louise would hang out. Jenny and Louise drank like fish and smoked weed like a furnace. Meanwhile, Mei Wei just sat and mostly listened.

"Well, y'all, come on in. We already got a full house, but I reckon you knew your momma told everybody she knew that you was coming." said a tipsy Uncle Frank.

While they headed inside, Ra'zee whispered to Mei Wei. "Hey beautiful, for the record, I apologize for not showing you more support in your job. You know I love you and would set the world on fire about you." Mei Wei lit up with the cheesiest smile ever. Ra'zee wrapped his arm around her waist, kissed her on the cheek, and continued, "Do yourself a favor by relaxing a little and enjoy yourself. Believe me, you deserve it."

She took a deep breath as if she was about to do a cannon ball jump into icy water for the first time, like Appolonia did in Purple Rain. Then she did something he had never seen her do before. She removed her glasses, put them in her coat pocket, and loosened her ponytail. Mei Wei's eyes sparkled like the ice capped edges of a glacier under a clear Alaskan sky at night.

Nervously and curiously, she asked, "How do I look babe?"

Ra'zee smiled pleasingly at her and said, "I've never seen anything more beautiful." She blushed and extended her hand so that he could help her keep her balance as she went up the snow dusted stairs.

Family and old friends were everywhere inside the house. Ra'zee thought that it looked more like an after party set from a club than a family get together. Mei Wei just smiled and nodded as Ra'zee re-introduced her to many in the room that didn't address her by name. His mom Alvona went back into the living room to finish playing her hand of cards, because everyone complained she had left too long and held up the game of Spades. It didn't take long for Ra'zee to find himself a Miller Draft beer. His crazy ass cousin Louise, who now stayed in Anoka, was walking around barefoot with a cup of E&J Brandy in one hand and a fifth of Wild Irish Rose under her arm. She had no problem drinking up somebody else's liquor, but her bottle was off limits. Shocked to see her barefoot in her momma's house, five and a half hours from Minnesota, Ra'zee went to Louise.

"Louise, when did you get down here? Last I heard, you was in St. Peters. My momma said it had something to do with a fight at the U of M campus in St. Paul? For the life of me, I still can't figure out what you were doing over there. You don't go to school over there."

Louise laughed loudly as she said, "Boy, I don't know. I was drunk at this party. Then I got into it with this girl because her man chose me. She better be glad campus security saved her, because I was about to cut her ass." Ra'zee loved Louise. Still, he couldn't help but think, "Who in the hell chose you at U of M?" She was twice popped on the ugly side, ghetto as hell, and her weave didn't match her hair.

Ra'zee looked down and said, "Girl, where the hell are your shoes?"

Louise looked down at her ashy feet and said, "Oh, I left them in the back. I was watching a movie in your old room."

Mei Wei glanced down and then looked away as she

said to herself, "If she didn't have no socks on and was in his bed, we going to the hotel." Then she said aloud to Louise, "Come on girl, let's go find your shoes. What movie was you watching?"

Louise didn't answer her but yelled over her shoulder to Jenny as she headed to the back, "Jenny, come keep me company. I'll share some of my bottle with you." As she scraped her bottle alongside the wall going down the hall, Louise told Mei Wei, "You know, my hair hang just like yours. I just need to get a touch up at the shop."

Jenny was very blunt spoken, a little ghetto, and smelled like a pound of weed and corner store perfume most of the time. She lightly tapped Mei Wei on the shoulder as she grunted and said, "Ain't no shop in Milwaukee gone help that patch on her head. She needs to just cut that off and start over." Mei Wei couldn't help but laugh a little when she heard that.

Inside the room, it was just as Mei Wei had feared. There crumpled up on a pillow, were Louise's dirty socks, loose change, and sunflower seed shells on the bedspread in a pile. Louise walked right up into the bed and then sat down. Jenny didn't care. She lit her little piece of a marijuana blunt and drank right out of the bottle with Louise. After she took a swig, she passed the bottle to Mei Wei who paused until she thought about what Ra'zee had said and how she wanted to please him. Her first sip didn't appear to be too nasty, so she took another and another and another as they talked. It wasn't long before all three of them were in the bed with their shoes off. Her and Jenny laughed as Louise told them story after story about her drama-filled life and trips to St. Peter's psychiatric hospital.

As the liquor kicked in, Mei Wei started to sweat so Louise loaned her a t-shirt right out of her Kmart suitcase, a rabbit eared shopping bag. It is scientifically known that Asians metabolize alcohol faster than any other ethnic group on the planet. Some believe that it is due to generations of a middle eastern diet high in amino acids and protein yet lean in fats. That, over the course of several millennia, changed their physical composition to fully process foods and libation quicker than most. Unlike some, the liquor would have taken three to four house to produce a high level of intoxication. Mei Wei was an animated drunk in less than two. Her attitude quickly changed from her normal quiet self to more of a gangster hood rich female like Griselda Blanco, a.k.a the cocaine godmother. Unlike Griselda ranting about her cartel enemies, Mei Wei talked about the dangerous vials, hazardous petri dishes, and cutthroat coworkers that she dealt with on the regular. Louise sat highly engaged into everything Mei Wei and acted as if she had witness all of these heinous plots against her and had actually tried to warn her about her coworkers. Jenny just laughed and kept drinking all of Louise's bottle. She knew that Mei Wei's ass was drunk. Since she loved to instigate bullshit everywhere she went, she thought it would be fun to witness how it would sit with Ra'zee once he found out that his goodie two shoe's princess had been corrupted. Like clockwork before the thought became a fleeting curiosity in her mind, Ra'zee came through the bedroom door.

"Mei Wei, hey beautiful, come take a picture with me, my mom, and Uncle Frank," he called before his eyes met her face.

"Decimal, tell them what I do babe. Tell them how these bitches at my job keep trying me. Oh, I bet if I chopped one of their heads off, I'd get some respect," Mei Wei said through hiccups and slurred speech.

Ra'zee asked adamantly, "What the fuck happen to you? What did y'all bitches give my wife?"

Mei Wei tried to stand up and tripped over Louise's ashy feet and fell smack dab into Ra'zee's chest.

CHAPTER 7
BIRTH OF A GREMLIN

S he regained her footing in the bed by using his shoulders for balance. Then, suddenly fear consumed her as she looked deeply into his dark brown eyes and replayed his initial request in her mind. After his words had climbed the rocky mountain side of drunken bullshit that she was talking about and reached the summit of sensibility, she smiled excitedly at the thought of taking pictures with him, his mom, and his Uncle Frank. Other than his proposal for marriage, she hadn't smiled at a thought like that in a very long time. As she looked up into Ra'zee's eyes and allowed the sun of reality of where she was, how she looked, and the fact that she was drunk wash over her, tears started to stream down her face.

"Help me down, I have to go pee," she said as she

struggled for balance. "Where is ma? Am I still pretty?"

Ra'zee thought to himself, "Her little ass is chopped. I know Louise ain't got the mental function to plot nothing like this. This has scandalous ass Jenny written all over it."

As he helped Mei Wei down, he glanced at Jenny. She cut her eyes at him and looked away with a smirk on her face. Ever since Uncle Frank had brought Jenny's trifling ass around the family and she caught wind that Decimal was his nephew, Jenny secretly saw herself as Mei Wei's replacement. Alvona easily saw right through her façade with Uncle Frank. Even though she remained polite to Jenny, Jenny knew that she didn't trust her.

Since the dawn of time, godless women have been the fabric of betrayal between man and morality. Right now, Jenny looked damn good sitting on his bed. Just like the mouthwatering fruit from the tree of knowledge of good and evil, in the midst of Eden, the Garden of God. When she knew that she had his full attention, she moved the pillow from her lap, stretched out fully on his bed, and let out a fake yawn. She arched her back fully so that he could see the imprint of her nipples that were like a stack of dimes under her blouse. Next, she stretched her legs all the way down to her toes to show off her curves, her toned muscles and the two-inch gap between her thighs. Meanwhile, Mei Wei had on a camouflaged g-unit t-shirt while her long blue jean skirt was twisted sideways. Her small front pocket was damn near on her butt, and she had on Louise's dirty white tube socks. One of her black nylon stockings were tied around her left bicep like an assassin and the other around her forehead like John Rambo. Ra'zee swallowed slow and hard as he looked away from Jenny. He grabbed Mei Wei's shirt and purse from the hook on the back of the door on their way out of the room. Jenny just stared at him.

The cool water on her face helped Mei Wei sober up a little. "I think I am going to be sick," she said through a queasy voice. "I am sorry, but can we go check into a hotel soon? I do not want to stay up all night with Louise and Jenny. We can come back early and have breakfast with your mom, "she pleaded.

Knowing that she wasn't used to drinking and was pretty lit, he said, "Of course beautiful. We should get a plate of barbeque off the stove on our way out. Trust me, cold barbeque is so good when you are hung over. Plus, you will need something to coat your stomach so that you don't get sick."

She sighed in relief and said, "Thanks babe." Then he hugged her from behind while they both looked in the mirror at each other. He couldn't help but laugh at how she looked in that wild wet hairstyle, wearing that g-unit t-shirt with that sweet, savage, sexy look in her eyes like the R&B singer Kehlani. Not long after he had started to laugh, she soon laughed too.

After a couple minutes, she asked, "So, how do you like my new look babe?"

Ra'zee kissed her on the top of the head and said,

"I am definitely feeling this new relaxed look. You probably could lose the g-unit t-shirt though. Especially since 50 Cent don't even wear g-unit t- shirts no more. Oh, and unless you want to end up like Louise, stop drinking that Wild Irish Rose. That bottle is known to breed drama. I like to see you enjoy yourself. I don't like to see you drunk off your ass and not even function. Feel me?" he asked sternly.

Sheepishly, she lowered her head and said, "You're right. Maybe I shouldn't drink?"

He said, "How about we have an occasional drink together at home or maybe at a restaurant. That would probably work better and give you more balance as far as your limits? Shit, you can't drink like Louise and Jenny. Hell, I can't drink like Louise and Jenny. All they do is drink!"

Mei Wei laughed as she thought about how all three of them were passing the bottle in bed.

"I must admit," his voice inflexion changed passionately. Her eyes held his gaze in the mirror for what seemed like an eternity.

Then, finally she said, "What is it babe? What?" Then she held her head to the side exposing the nape of her neck. With one hand around her waist, he pressed tightly against her as an intense sexual urge took hold of him. He lowered his head until his lips found her ear lobe.

"Mei Wei," he whispered as he gently bit her on the neck.

"Yes Ra'zee" she responded as she gasped for air and rose up onto the tips of her toes.

"Mugwhy, I sense both passion and aggression in you. Show me more."

That's when it hit her. A feeling of liberation coursed through her veins and suddenly she felt new; different and alive. It was as if a door had unlocked, and she saw a jazzy, bad bitch step out. She not only held the attention of her husband, but everybody else in the room. The desire to lead a quiet life, mind her own business and work with her own hands left her swiftly. A rollercoaster of wild ideas flooded her mind as she latched onto the thought of being the baddest bitch in the room. For several millennia, liquor has been called by many names. Universally, it has always been known as a cup of courage. Whatever phobias she had about losing her husband, or the street life was conquered in the blink of an eye.

She turned toward him and challenged with sexual flare in her eyes, "You want to see more gremlin Decimal? Kick Louise and Jenny out of your room for about fifteen minutes."

Ra'zee picked her up, sat her on the sink, and stepped in between her legs. Immediately she stripped off Louise's t-shirt and wrapped her legs around her waist. She pulled off each sock with her toes and dropped them with the t-shirt in a pile on the floor.

As he leaned in to kiss her, she placed a hand on his chest and said, "You're going to have to wait until later.

Plus, don't we have pictures to go take with ma and Uncle Frank?"

He tried to lean in to kiss her again. As she placed one finger on his lips to say no, Jenny walked in the bathroom. When she saw Mei Wei with her shirt off and her legs wrapped around Ra'zee waist, she jealously said, "Get a room."

Mei Wei snapped back, "Keep it real Jenny. You wish you could be me. You think I don't smell your bullshit through all of that cheap ass perfume you wear. You'd better get you some business before I have to get in that ass." Then she pushed Ra'zee out of the way and jumped down off the sink. He grabbed her as she muffed Jenny in the face. Jenny stumbled back into the hall and Mei Wei closed the door.

Ra'zee's mom came down the hallway just as the bathroom door closed. Even though she saw and heard everything, she asked, "Is someone in the bathroom?"

Jenny tried to downplay the whole incident and said, "Yes ma'am, your son and his wife are in there. I think that she has an upset stomach."

Alvona turned around and walked off. While going down the hall, she smiled and said low under her breath, "So my daughter finally got tired of yo ass huh?"

Jenny asked, "What did you say?"

Alvona replied in a cynical tone, "Oh nothing, I just said I'll come back in a minute."

Jenny looked furious at her. Uncle Frank met Alvona at the end of the hall and said, "Honey, you are holding the card game up again."

She said, "I am coming, I needed to use the bathroom."

Uncle Frank smiled at Jenny and said, "Say, darling, you want some barbeque now?"

Feeling quite embarrassed, Jenny said, "I am ready to go," rolled her eyes and headed down the hall past Uncle Frank. Uncle Frank looked shocked as to why she wanted to leave so suddenly.

Thinking that she probably felt left out, he asked her, "What's wrong Jenny? You mad at me?"

Visually irritated and feeling disgusted with herself, and at the fact that Uncle Frank was a really good guy and that it was his fault that he wanted to leave, she said, "I forgot that I need to get up early. Can you please just drop me off? I am really sorry about everything Frank. If need be, I guess I could just catch a cab. I know that you haven't seen your nephew in a while and want to spend some time with him."

Uncle Frank responded sympathetically and said, "Now now, that won't be necessary. Just let me grab my keys. I will take you."

Jenny walked off down the hall and replied coldly to his offer, "I'll be outside in the car."

Louise came out of the bedroom as Uncle Frank headed down the hall behind Jenny. When she noticed Uncle Frank reach for his keys, thoughts of a fast mode of transportation to her next bottle crossed her mind.

"Hey, Uncle Frank. Where you going?" she asked

him.

Uncle Frank knew that nine times out of ten, Louise wanted him to take her somewhere too. That more than likely she needed another bottle and didn't have enough money. Before she could pry him for more information, he plainly said, "Louise, come and take a ride with your uncle. Jenny has got an appointment early in the morning and I need to drop her off. I'll buy you a bottle."

She yelled, "Okay, let me grab my shoes!" With no socks on and only one of her shoes in sight, she grabbed an old pair of Ra'zee's work boots from the closet and left.

Ra'zee held Mei Wei's hand as she pushed him out of the bathroom and towards his old bedroom door. Not knowing that the room was empty, he paused as he twisted the doorknob and whispered to her like a nervous teen sneaking his high school sweetheart past his mom "What am I supposed to tell them? It's a full house."

Mei Wei hunched, grunted twice like a cave woman, cleared her throat, then smacked him on the butt and said, "Get in there Decimal or do you need this little gremlin to make a scene?"

He laughed lightly through his whispers as he peeked over his shoulder at her and said, "What has gotten into you?"

She lightly stomped her feet in response to his question, grunted twice again like a cave woman, and pointed at the door.

Ra'zee hit his chest like a caveman and said, "Woman, watch. Me, man get room for you now." They both laughed as he opened the door and said, "You two, excuse us for a minute..." Then they noticed the room was empty. He stepped in and asked her suspiciously, "I wonder where those two went?"

He turned around as he heard the door close behind them and the bolt latch slide into place. Mei Wei held a hungry sexual look in her eyes as she unhooked her bra and threw it at him. She pushed him back onto the bed and jumped on top of him as she said, "Who in the hell cares where they went? Hurry up and make love to me before they come back!"

Ra'zee smiled as they rolled over and said, "Now that's what I am talking about. I think that I am really going to like this new side of you." She unzipped her skirt and slid out of it as they rolled over several more times in bed. She moaned a short gasp behind each soft kiss as he inched his way down her stomach. Quickly, she reached for a pillow to bite as he placed her left foot on his right shoulder and savored the sticky salt-like taste beyond her lace panties between her thighs. Her sweaty hands quickly found the top of his head as she lifted her right leg high into the air and pulled his face deeper into her love.

As she climaxed, she whispered, "Sex is so much better with liquor."

His muffled response rose up from between her

thighs and said, "I know. I know."

PART 2: SEEDS OF DAMNATION

CHAPTER 8
INNOCENT TEARS

———— ⊶⦵⧓⦵⊷ ————

McIntyre's experience told heart that the woman on the other end of the phone was amid a psychotic break. "Ma'am, I need you to calm down. Can you please tell me your name, where you are at and the name of your tending psychiatrist?" she asked with concern in her voice. While McIntyre waited for an answer, she checked to see what emergency mental health staff was available onsite at the hospital. Preferably a therapist that may be better equipped to handle this call.

Tears streamed down Maria's face as she choked back heavy sobs and yelled into the phone, "Carmen, it's me Maria! Did you not just hear what I said? Something is wrong with Carlos." Confused as to what was wrong with his mom Jaysaiah cried as Rita and Katherine walked into the room. Maria continued to sob frustrated into the phone. "I know that we haven't spoken in a very long time, but I need you. I can't shake the feeling that something is terribly wrong. That something awful is about to happen. That somehow Carlos is at the center of it all. He has started to act very strange, more strange than usual. I had to call because I didn't know what else to do and I don't have anyone that I can trust to talk to."

It had been almost two years since she heard someone else speak Carlos's name. Almost three years since the nightmares stopped. Almost four years since the police department leaks mixed with media speculation made her a captive in her own home. Silently, she fell into a catatonic-like state and blacked out. The phone receiver slipped from her hand, and she watched as it fell in slow motion for what seemed like an eternity until it hit the counter then the floor. She acutely heard water vibrations behind the force of the thud that rippled through her bottle by the computer monitor. Hypnotized, she allowed each ripple that expanded across the shallow water, to mentally take her back in time. Like a strong current pulling her out to sea, they swept her away to a simpler time before the darkness invaded her life. The last time she saw Carlos' face to face in their Rosemont home shot through her mind like a runaway freight train and her emotions quickly ran out of tracks. The images slammed into her psyche with a debilitating force and choked her ability to breathe. Fear mixed with joy at the possibility of seeing Carlos soon.

Her heart tensed as she recalled the words of the Widow Maker. How he told her that one day he would return Carlos to her. At the appointed season when penance must be taught again. Worry fell heavily like cold dirt upon her heart and buried all of her hopes as the realization of what seeing her only son again might mean for his safety. Her heart pounded as tiny beads of sweat formed down the nape of her neck. The pupils of her eyes dilated as the hairs on her arms prickled and rose. She knew she would vomit soon as vapors of acid rose in her stomach and reached the back of her throat. A wintry chill touched her bones, grabbed her voice box, and stole her ability to speak. When Misty came back by the nurse's station to get a patient's chart, McIntyre just sat there, wide eyes in shock at the desk. Huge gum drop-like tears hung from her long dark eyelashes and Misty couldn't help but notice something was terribly wrong.

"McIntyre, what is it? What's wrong?" Misty pleaded through concerned whispers.

McIntyre didn't so much as even look up at Misty, let alone try to speak. Her silence birthed a weird aura that surrounded the nurse's station and drew the attention of several passing patients along with medical personnel in the hall. Upon noticing this, Misty quickly went behind the desk, took McIntyre by the hand, and pulled her into the supervisor's office. She instinctively closed the blinds that covered the two side windows for privacy.

As she reached for the pull string to close the blinds that covered the small window on the door, she noticed the phone receiver from the desk off the console on the floor. She searched McIntyre's face for some sign of coherent mental awareness. After she didn't see one and quickly assessed that she would be fine by herself momentarily, she lightly rubbed McIntyre's shoulder for comfort.

Then, she warmly said, "Wait here, I will be right back."

McIntyre slowly swam back through the mental fog of shock to reality. Meanwhile, Misty's eyes darted back and forth from the information on the computer monitor to McIntyre behind the door. She carefully studied both as she picked up the phone from the floor to try to figure out who was on the line and what department aids had last been looked up. Above all, she really wanted to know what had made McIntyre freeze up. McIntyre had always been a display of great composure in the midst of the most difficult situations that she had ever witnessed at Regions Hospital. On one occasion, two parents had come running into the emergency room crying hysterically while yelling for help. The husband and the wife were soaked in the blood of their only daughter, whose body hung lifelessly limp as the father carried her in her arm. She was a mere toddler who had a self-inflicted gunshot wound to the abdomen from an unsecured loaded handgun that she found in the house. They had witnessed a victim wake up from a freak car accident, who became terrified and had to be sedated after he saw the pints of blood bags on his lap next to the tree branch. That was still wedged in the right side of his torso, and he tried to get off the gurney. Others were heart wrenching encounters that some doctors with parents suffering from Alzheimer's couldn't stomach. They had dealt with emotionally abandoned suicidal elderly patients without family or loved ones to care for them because they were choosing rather to live their lives instead. McIntyre had always led the charge of first responders at Regions Hospital. She showed great resolve to make tough life- saving decisions in microseconds while under intense pressure.

It was puzzlingly odd to Misty that someone like McIntyre, who had typically shown such resilience in the face of horrendous circumstances, that a mere phone call reduced her to a gnome's existence. To withdraw from reality and guard her most sacred treasure, her mind. Whatever that call had just revealed happened to be so earth shattering that when she heard it, she instantly became unglued. Misty took a deep breath, exhaled slowly, and then suspiciously spoke into the phone as she watched McIntyre.

"Thank you for holding, this is Region Hospital fourth floor nurses' station. My name is Misty. How may I assist you or direct your call?"

Maria instantly became distracted from her sniffling and exhaustive crying and asked, "What? Who is this? What did you say? Where is Carmen?"

Misty responded, "RNT McIntyre was needed elsewhere. Is there something that I can help you with?"

Maria didn't say another word and simply hung up the phone. Misty responded to the silence with several, "Hello, ma'am are you there?" requests. When no reply was heard, she looked awkwardly at the phone receiver, then McIntyre for a brief moment. Then, with a suspicious look on her face, as if to say, "I am going to get to the bottom of this," she hung up the phone and went back to check on her best friend.

Maria slowly closed the phone screen on her iPhone. Frustrated, she stared out of the window at the plush pasture of her uncle's land and said, "Dammit Carmen."

Mei Wei and Ra'zee exited the bedroom just as his youngest aunt named Carlotta took off the old school Betty Wright, "No Pain No Gain" album and started playing Kehlani. Mei Wei was really feeling herself after her session with Ra'zee, so she came out of the bedroom barefoot in a skimpy pair of shorts. She had on Ra'zee's custom made Milwaukee Buck's jersey that had his nickname "Decimal" on the back. She grabbed two bottles of Miller Draft from the refrigerator. Then, while singing Kehlani's song "Distraction", she started to dance sexy on Ra'zee and he was loving it. No one in the family had ever seen this side of her and they instantly knew something was very different about her. Before long, she grabbed the Amsterdam vodka bottle from the open shelf of liquor bottles on the walk-in kitchen countertop. The song changed to "Crazy", and Mei Wei started dancing just like Kehlani from the video: sweet, savage, and sexy-like. Their dance game escalated as the family cheered and Ra'zee literally became nothing more than a distraction from her having the spotlight.

She abruptly stopped her playful bad girl Kehlani routine as she fixed and slammed a shot of vodka. Her face tightened immediately, along with squinted eyes and creased lips behind the strong bite of liquor on her throat. A warm shiver rolled over her like heat from an oven. The 40-proof alcoholic beverage coursed rapidly through her veins, abducted the remainder of her morals, and destroyed the last of her innocence. She ran to the bedroom and grabbed her iPod. As she came back into the living room, she didn't even look at Ra'zee. She slightly pushed through him and clawed his chest in desperation. Her body language playfully said, "Let me have this moment to myself, I will be back." Ra'zee walked over and stood by Uncle Frank who had just returned with Louise from dropping Jenny off. Mei Wei held up her hand and then extended a finger to everyone to beckon that they please give her one moment, like she had something special in store for them as she turned the CD off. Everyone smiled and grew quiet as they intently watched her, except for Louise's crazy ass who just loudly complained that the previous song was her jam. Alvona hushed everyone as Mei Wei placed her iPod on the dock connected to the stereo. She selected a soulful, primarily acoustic guitar song about a girl who had lost her true identity and didn't know how to get it back by Kip Moore called, "Blonde."

She then started this exotic Asian enchantress dance as she poured and refilled several empty glasses at the main table. Ra'zee sensed instantly that she had long since stopped dancing for him, but for the attention of everyone else in the room. He tried to pull her close to dance with, but Mei Wei gently pulled away with a spiteful look in her eyes like that of a caged rebellious geisha whore that said, "Everybody out of the pool, the mother fucking lifeguard is off duty!"

In that very moment, Mei Wei looked away from Ra'zee but not before their eyes briefly locked and he read all of the pain in her soul. How she had sacrificed her family, her heritage, and even her mother for him. That in return, he still wasn't satisfied and wanted more. The look of spite had also underscored the fact that she had given all she was going to give and that it was her turn to receive and that he had better find a way to accommodate her new lifestyle or adjust to a new lifestyle at home without her. Mei Wei looked away as she danced. She closed her eyes and thought about her family that had cut her off because she loved Ra'zee. In specific, she thought about her mother, who fed her when she was a child, wiped her eyes when she cried, let her play dress up in her clothes, made her feel special and now had stood passively by her father-in-law and disowned her. That's when an overwhelmed Mei Wei felt the hottest blast of heat she had ever felt behind the combination of liquor and dehydration. She lost all controlled motion in her legs and stumbled several times in the midst of her very graceful routine.

They say that a mother knows their child best. While her husband stood there, Alvona's eyes widened like a freshly mint Susan B Anthony one dollar coin. She stood quicky and dropped her drink as she yelled, "Ra'zee, get her, she's about to faint."

As Decimal sprinted to catch his wife, Mei Wei spiraled as she collapsed in the center of the floor and fell into his arms.

CHAPTER 9
FLOWERS IN THE ATTIC

———————◇◦⃝◦◇———————

Several strips of soiled pink asbestos covered insulation pads showed beneath the missing floorboards in the spacious attic. The remains of an old phonograph sat in the corner with a cracked record caked by dirt on the top of it. A partially burned mirror lay on its side in the corner that only contained a few pieces of jagged charred glass left in it. An outdated pair of light blue, hard bottomed baby shoes from the 1920's were tied together by its shoestrings. Opposite the shoes, by the arch of the wall in a faint cast of flickering storm light, there was a stick figure drawing of what appeared to be twin girls with freckles names Magdalene and Marybeth. Below the picture, next to a bent pair of metal toddlers leg braces, were several dirty alphabet letter blocks along with large wooden puzzle pieces. A heavy old black iron trunk sat mysteriously in the center of the floor. It bore what appeared to be some type of cast iron family crescent lock fastened through heavy straps that secured it to the floor. The image on the lock closely resembled the signet from a ring that would officiate a document before it was placed at the entrance of a crypt, like it was to seal away a sarcophagus by a ruling council. After that judgment had been issued, authority would be given to lock away some dark evil or person for eternity.

A casing of shed snakeskin, a cat's paw on a chain linked to some type of talisman along with a large crow's feather covered the floor in front of a key that was an Aramaic symbol on an eight-point pentagram etched by white chalk on the floor. Fragments of burnt candles sat in thirteen symbol-marked places around the outer edge of the circle. These were markings that indicated someone had attempted to invoke, possess, and bind some kind of spirit through some sort of cultic seance.

The Widow Maker seethed in a low voice, "Hairless monkeys, always tampering with forces you can't possibly understand." He proceeded towards the box in the middle of the floor to open it. The Widow Maker stopped with the toes of his shoes at the edge of the chalk line after he noticed the oil-stained circle burned lightly into the floor at the very center of the pentagram. Carlos's eyes split in the outer corners revealing a smaller set of pupils in each eye looking out.

"An angel trap! Why I haven't seen one of you in a

very long time," he hissed. Slowly, he began walking backwards to the door while looking around and continued, "Tsk. Tsk... Tsk... I wonder who revealed such knowledge to you? Even more, is there actually a foolish guest in there that somehow allowed their name at creation to be discovered and used by a decadent cult to entrap them? Interesting. Still, there will be no entrapments today. For we have much work to do. Hmm, now I am curious as to what other secrets does Stonewall Plantation hold?"

When Carlos exited the attic, the hallway was completely empty. Still, he couldn't shake the overwhelming sensation that a pair of eyes watched his every step. Suddenly, he began to hear the familiar chime of six nickels falling to the ground as his vision grew hazy.

The Widow Maker smiled and said, "A foolish woman is clamorous. She is simple and knows nothing," as Ms. Hatchfield appeared out of nowhere with her back to him and headed down the hall, she had come out of one of the many sliding panels that gave cloaked passage through the crawl space, parallel to the corridors, between the bedroom walls and the halls. Passageways that she had used on several occasions to torment Stonewall Plantations overnight guests to get them to believe in the hoodoo that's commonly practiced in the bayous. Over the years, she had tricked numerous individuals into believing that they were in terrible, spiritual danger by making strange child-like noises in their bedrooms at night such as clapping, giggling, running or bouncing a ball. She usually did this inside the crawl space behind their closet or by the bathtub while they soaked in their private bathroom, under candlelight during late hours of the night. When terror gripped them and their hearts exploded in panic, she miraculously appeared to counsel them and provide the help that they desperately needed.

Having personally been the instrument of fear for several millennia, he was privy to the game that she was attempting to initiate. The Widow Maker smiled delightedly wrathful at her with thoughts of drinking her soul from his chalice of torture. Then, he played possum, acted as if he was the typical bewitched visitor that she had baited in the past and said, "Oh, I am glad it's you Ms. Hatchfield. Something strange is going on up here. I think that someone, something is in the house. I thought I heard the sound of whispering coming from that room." He then pointed to the closed attic door that he had just come out of. Ms. Hatchfield turned around and looked mockingly suspicious at Carlos and then the attic door. With a fake startled look of caution, she stepped between him and the door to lead him back into the room. As soon as she walked inside the room and walked across the pentagram, each of Carlos's eyes split as he closed the door while peeking down the hall. When the second set of small pupils passed from behind his original ones to the outer corner of his eyes, like the molecular splitting of an atom. Carlos's eyes became spotted with dark orange spots like the skin of a leopard.

The Widow Maker walked up behind her as she said, "Are you sure it was in here? It seems pretty quiet in here."

The Widow Maker whispered dryly, "Not for long," and pushed Ms. Hatchfield in the back with such force that she tripped and fell headfirst into the black box strapped to the floor. When old man Stonewall, who was still downstairs in his wheelchair by the grandfather clock, heard the loud crack from upstairs, he looked up at the ceiling and started to ring his help bell on his wheelchair. Her head hit the box and broke it free from the straps. Both slid across the floor which destroyed the barrier marking of the pentagram and tumbled on their sides by the window. Slowly, she crawled away as she left a blood trail behind her. The six-inch gash in her forehead was a repulsive bright pink bowl shaped crater. The missing chunk of flesh revealed exposure down to the cranial bone. Desperately, she clawed at the floor and tried to pull herself into a corner. Downstairs, old man Stonewall's eyes continued to stare up at the ceiling. Terrified, he followed Carlos's footsteps as he moved across the floor behind her. Frantically, his finger twitched as he mumbled and rang the help bell on his wheelchair.

"Ring, ring, ring, ring, ring.. Mm, mmm.. Ring, ring, ring, ring.. Mmm, mm!"

The Widow Maker looked piercingly down through

the floor when he heard the bell and said, "Don't worry, I will be down shortly to discuss the vacancy of your personal caretaker position. It appears that Ms. Hatchfield here has other long-term plans on her mind."

She grabbed hold of the leg of an old dresser and tried to use it to stand. Half dazed, she stuttered, trembled, and cried as the realization that her attacker had just begun settled in and her bowels let loose. A torrid scent washed off from the watery fluid of stool and urine that mixed as it poured forth from her body. Thick, lime green and yellow snot caked her nostrils as she offered the weak form of a plea, "Pl-ple-please stop..." she begged.

The Widow Maker broke apart one of the old metal leg braces and twisted it into a jagged dagger. With a violent thrust, he plunged the contorted metal into her back, between her shoulder blades, and cracked two vertebrae discs in her spine. Her eyes filled with fear and bulged as the excruciating pain that preceded her paralysis laid hold of her mind. The Widow Maker held his head back as his back arched in a primal stretch. His eyes rolled into the back of his head as he exhaled an asthmatic shuttered breath that matched her strangulation- like cry. He drank her life force like sweet tea as it left her body. Then, he forcefully cracked several more vertebrae and cut through the flesh in her back like a tough piece of steak with a dull knife.

While she violently twitched, he leaned into her ear

and whispered sadistically through a panting breath, "Stop your squirming. The Light of Death is upon you! The wolf does not negotiate with the lamb. Therefore, I will not spare, show pity or remorse."

When she lay totally limp, he pulled the jagged metal from her back and wiped it off on the edge of her dingy violet flowered sleeping gown. Next, he took the three large wooden alphabet lettered blocks and forced them down between the fractured vertebrae of her spine. With each lettered block that he forced into the cavity with his bare hand, he grunted a solitary word. "A-aa is for Abaddon, the Destroyer of Worlds. B-ee is for Belial, Lawlessness. C is for Chemosh, the Subduer." He set the heavy black box upright and twisted the lock with the metal piece until it broke off. He contorted Ms. Hatchfield's body as he stuffed her into the box until her right foot was on the side of her face. He stared deep into her bulging, terror filled eyes as he closed the lid on the box and whispered to her, "I must admit, you are far more flexible than you look."

Then, he looked over his shoulder at the sound of the bell and mumbling that came from downstairs. "ring, ring, ring... Mm, mm!.. Ring, ring, ring, ring... Mmm, mmm!"

He looked back at the contorted corpse in the box and said, "I would love to stay and chat, but someone has to go and tend to old Henry Lee Stonewall. And since your schedule is full..." He paused with a mock look of surprise and burden, shrugged his shoulders, and finished, "Well, I guess that leaves me?" Then, he closed the lid on the box.

He got to the door, paused at a simple thought, then turned around and went back to box. He opened the lid and said, "Oh, I almost forgot. You'll need a fee for the Boatman." With the jagged tip of the twisted metal leg brace, he gouged out her eyes and jammed three nickels into each eye socket, slammed the lid on the box and left.

When old man Stonewall heard the creak of the floorboards from the weight of footsteps that came back across the floor of the attic, he stopped ringing the bell on his wheelchair and became very quiet and still. The Widow Maker descended the steps slowly. He paused slightly on each step while he held a deathly gaze on the old man who sat still by the grandfather clock. He lightly wrapped his fingernails on the banister during his descent until he came and stood behind Henry Lee Stonewall. Old man Stonewall said nothing as he sat partially frozen in his wheelchair and tried to look out of the corner of his eye behind him. The Light of Death stood there and contemplated what to do to him while he rolled a highly polished nickel down the miniature staircase of his knuckles over and over again. Then, it dawned on him of who would be a suitable replacement for Ms. Hatchfield. None other than the esteemed professor of rare psychological case studies Dr. Marcus Rutowski.

The Widow Maker smiled deathly at him as he stepped

around the right side of his wheelchair into full view. Old Henry Lee Stonewall gasped and lightly vomited in his mouth when he looked into the grotesque face of Animus, Egyptian Blackness, the Widow Maker. The right side of his face was seared flesh as if burned by a passing bolt of lightning. His jawline partly covered in flesh revealed a blackened gum line with a small gray maggot that slithered from between two of his teeth. His right eye, although chalk gray, depicted a level of coherent, methodical alertness that spoke of great intellect with baffling ingenuity. He waved at him with a pinky finger as he flipped the coin past his dead eye, winked, and crossed back by mirror into a dark abyss.

CHAPTER 10
DYING DREAMS

⊸∘◖⁘◗∘⊷

His bedroom at the retirement home was quiet and adorned with decorative furnishings. Several ceremonial musical instruments leaned in a corner next to a picture of his wife on a stand. Thin strips of white paper mulberry twirled from the ceiling by strings. Written on each strip in calligraphy was the name Bodhisattva (a future Buddha, who out of compassion forges nirvana, in order to save others). A bamboo wind chime rapped lightly against the window seal from the gentle breeze that came through the cracked window. An old tea pot from an earlier dynasty sat steaming on the countertop next to matching lid covered teacups. Three large wood and paper fans decorated the walls in a beautiful arrangement to remind him of his homeland and the ways of his people. Known by those closest to him as Yawg-Suab (The oldest living male Hmong descendant) and as the head of one of the eighteen royal families, Ip Vang lay quiet and still in his bed. His daughter Youa Wei Vang-Lee kneeled reverently in honor at his bedside.

Through a faint hoarse voice, Ip spoke to her in the Mao-Yao language from the mountainous region of southern China. He told her how important it was to reconcile her differences of opinion with her daughter Mei Wei Vang. That the old traditions of their homeland could not serve them best in this new one. He reminded her of what the Chinese philosopher Confucius wrote in that, "The gem cannot be polished without friction, nor man perfected without trial." If they were truly to grow generation after generation, that some things would have to change. In this case, especially the practice of exiling their family for the offense of violating tradition by dating outside of their race for love. Ip further reminded her of how he was scrutinized for dating an American woman long after her mother had died. That the friendship had helped him to heal and that he regretted giving in to pressure from the other family heads to not see her anymore. Although their traditions are important, Mei Wei is still Vang and cannot survive without her family. Even he had forsaken tradition and made peace with the Hmong Lee family for the sake of her marriage after years of family bitterness. Youa Wei said nothing as she wept in silence. She had missed her only child terribly over the last three and a half years. Out of tradition, she had once felt it was her place to stand by her stubborn husband's side.

Now, she felt different. It all began after that he had forbidden Mei Wei to see or talk to Ra'zee again because he was not Hmong and especially because he was African- American. Still, after sneaking around with him for several months, of which Mei Wei knew that her parents were aware of, she defiantly hoped her stepfather would change his mind after seeing how happy she was. Bashfully, she waited until after dinner to show them her engagement ring and asked for their blessing in marriage. Enraged, her stepfather slapped her and knocked her coke bottle thick glasses from her face. Then, he flipped the dinner table onto its side and dragged Mei Wei out of the house onto the front porch in the rain. Huge tear drops welled up in her dark oceanic blue eyes as he looked deeply into them disgusted and closed the door in her face. All the strength left her body as she beat on the door and cried in the rain. Youa Wei sat there and said nothing. Then, her heart cracked after hearing her precious daughter scream for her, "Momma, please!" and begged her to let her back inside. Cowardly, she ran from the dinner table and locked herself in Mei Wei's bedroom. She curled up in a fetal position on Mei Wei's bed and cried painfully while she hugged her daughters' pillow and smelled her scent for the last time.

Ra'zee pulled up in less than five minutes to get Mei

Wei after she had used the neighbor's house phone to call him. When he pulled up, she was sitting in the driveway, shielded by the house against the rain and shivering from the cold. She had on a soaking wet pair of long black kick boxing shorts, a snug fitting white t-shirt that revealed her hot pink bra, and mismatched orange slice and kiwi green colored ankle socks. She had stopped crying but started again as soon as Ra'zee helped her up. He quickly wiped the rain from her face, took his heavy hooded coat off and wrapped it around her. Ra'zee held her protectively in his arms as she looked back at the house and sobbed loudly while he walked her to the car. Youa Wei listened as the car door opened and cringed when it shut. Mei Wie moved in with Ra'zee that night and never came back for her things. Devastated by her mother's silence, they hadn't spoken since.

Youa Wei knew that her father Ip Vang loved her, but she still felt a little embarrassed by the underlying tone and meaning of his words, which were summed up by what Buddha said in that, "There are three things which cannot long be hidden. The sun, the moon, and the truth." This meant that she was basically being a hypocrite. Here, she had begged her father for mercy and had not shown any to her daughter. Even more so was the irony that the same man that she had faced exile for to be with had now exiled her daughter. Ip Vang's assigned nurse aid Sing came into the room and stood quietly by the door in respect for their privacy.

Ip Vang said to Youa Wei, "Daughter, it's getting close to lunch time. Will you be staying, or do you have other plans to tend to?"

Youa Wei looked solemnly at her father who still lay with his eyes closed. She reached out and placed her hand on top of his in loving affection, then whispered back, "Father, I do have other things to tend to. First, I need to go home and rest. I will come back in the morning though and let you know what Xiao Lee said after we talk tonight at dinner. Still, you are right. Mei Wei is Vang, and she has been away from our family for far too long. I just hope it's not too late, especially for her and I."

After several slow deep coughs, Ip Vang replied to Youa Wei while Sing came to his bedside, "Very well daughter. Please keep me informed as to if you need my assistance?"

Youa Wei stood and bowed slightly to her father in reverence. Then, she smiled at Sing on her way out of the room. On her way home, Yoa Wei stopped at an Asian aromatic store to get two candles and a dove's feather. In times of deep thought, she practiced a form of eastern mysticism that transcended her level of consciousness to obtain much needed enlightenment. She sat in front of the two candles in deep meditation with her feet in a basin of water. She fanned herself with a dove's feather and stared into the eyes of her Siamese house cat. She believed the dove to be the bird of heaven and the cat's eyes saw the spirit realm which would transport her to nirvana. There, she would be provided a doorway to see her ancestors through the candles so that she could gather secret knowledge from them.

In her mind's eye, she watched when the portal opened between the two candles. She saw nothing at first, but felt a strong presence preceded by a gust of wind on her face that smelled of blood and dead rodents. Suddenly, she heard the sound of hard sole dress shoes that approached from the distance. Terror struck her as she heard a wrathful voice that echoed from down what seemed to be an endless corridor of blinding light, "Lux Ab Exitium Velle Venere." Her trance was broken by the sound of Xiao Lee coming through the back door from work. She could tell that he was in a good mood based off the whistling that she heard in the kitchen. Xiao Lee nodded as Youa Wei bowed slightly to greet him.

"How was your day at work husband?" she asked in a low voice.

His smile changed to a serious expression as he removed his jacket and swung it onto a chair at the kitchen table. "It went by just fine wife," he said searchingly as he waited for her to look him in the eyes. When her eyes arose from the floor, a tear welled up in the corner of the right one.

Youa Wei's lips began to quiver as she said, "Husband, I saw Yawg- Suab today."

Xiao Lee quickly leaned in toward her with concern

on his face and asked, "Is he okay?"

She nodded several times rapidly as she said, "Yes, he is doing well."

He asked, "Well, what is it then that's bothering you? Is it something I did or can fix?"

Youa Wei replied, "We can talk about it later."

There have been bitter moments in every family. Things that were said on both sides of the isle in the heat of the moment that later were wished had not been said. Things that loved ones have done to each other in a split-second decision that has cost them a dear relationship for the rest of their lives. Sometimes, the act of betrayal is so brutal, so hurtful, and so unbelievable that it leaves a nasty scar on one's mind. A scar that can only be seen briefly, in a microsecond by a glance with the passing eye through the window of the soul. As Youa Wei's eyes slowly rose from the floor again, she briefly looked at Xiao Lee for a split second out of the corner of her right eye. He instantly knew once he looked into her eyes that she and Yawg- Suab had talked about Mei Wei.

In his heart, he had long since known he had made a bad decision to kick her out of the house. His hope of Mei Wei being a traditional girl when all she has ever known was America, St. Paul Minnesota to be exact, was pointless. He felt like he had a great responsibility in being the first marriage between the Hmong Lee and Hmong Vang families. His father had taught him to never be indecisive and stand firmly behind every decision that he made. People who could not make up their mind were not meant to rule, but to serve. He had chosen him over his brothers to be head of the Hmong Lee family, before his birth rite, because his brothers were lost in Western culture. Living in his father's shadow after he had died had been difficult. Often, he got lost in his father's identity, which made it difficult for him to be married to the daughter of Ip Vang. He wished his father had taught him to be more compassionate and to repent. Xiao Lee sat Youa Wei in a chair. He kneeled in front of her and hugged her while she looked at the floor and cried.

He kissed her on top of her head and said in a low compassionate voice, "Worry not about dinner wife. Go and find your daughter Mei Wei. I will not go with you for I am bound by my word to my father Hsin Lee. To stand firm with my decisions that I make as head of this family. However, you have my blessing to see Mei Wei, just not here." Youa Wei smiled through her tears as he finished, "Maybe one day Mei Wei and I can reconcile if she shows respect to the decision that I made after we gave her ample time to accept her place in our family and way of life. Enough said, you go, and I hope you find her."

Youa Wei held her husband's face as she sighed in relief. Her eyes suddenly lit up as the torch of new life appeared to burn in each one of them and she saw a path to her daughter again. Faintly, she whispered, "Thank you husband. I am going to change my clothes and go to her house. I will be back soon."

As she hurried out of the kitchen, Xiao Lee asked, "You know where to find her?"

Youa Wei didn't even turn around as she ran up the stairs and said, "She is my daughter, I have always known where she was at."

Xiao Lee had just finished steaming some tea leaves in a cup when he heard Youa Wei go out the front door. Thoughts of how close Mei Wei had been all this time crossed his mind. What kind of life did she live and was she in any kind of trouble now?

It took Youa Wei about fifteen minutes to reach Mei Wei and Ra'zee's Maplewood home. She felt sad to learn that no one was there. So, she left a note with her number on the door that said, "Daughter please call me, love Mom" and headed back home to take a nap.

CHAPTER 11
NOTES FROM THE PAST

When Mei Wei woke up the following morning, she was laying alone in Ra'zee's bed. She heard the sound of him and his mom laughing in the kitchen through the cracked bedroom door. Quietly, she eased out of bed and closed the bedroom door. She climbed back in bed, wrapped the sheet around her shoulders and pulled her knees up into her chest. She stared out of the window at the brightness of the sun that reflected from the sheet of ice-covered snow on the lawn. Huge Ice age sickles spearheaded from the rain gutters. Slowly, she recalled last night, her physical confrontation with Jenny, and her collapse in front of everyone. Humorous embarrassment washed over her, and she couldn't help to laugh. She whispered to herself, "Gir-rl, what the hell is wrong with you? This is crazy! Oh well, Ra'zee asked for this, so it is what it is. I just got to keep it together. Don't want to get too wild. But still, I had a lot of fun last night. Might as well go in here and sit with ma before we leave later."

Mei Wei peaked around the corner of the kitchen doorway with one eye on Alvona. Alvona smoked her cigarette and laughed with Ra'zee, Uncle Frank, and Jesse at Louise's crazy ass St. Peter's hospital stories. She told them about the guards stealing her chicken money, then how her new doctor Dr. Rutowski liked her and was going to give her electric therapy so that they could be together. Alvona laughed so hard that tears fell from her eyes.

She said, "Louise, shut the hell up before you make me pee myself listening to yo crazy ass. That doctor wants to shock some sense into your ass, not be with you."

Louise picked her bottle up from off of the floor, next to her ashy feet, and said, "Un, un... he do like me. That's why he wants to see me all of the time."

Alvona cut in with a gasp for air while she laughed hard and said, "He keeping a close eye on you just in case he need to put your butt in impatient care."

Louise scratched her head as she tucked her bottle under her arm and said, "As long as they pay for it. Ooo, some of those places are really nice. Plus, the staff take me everywhere I need to go."

Alvona wiped her eyes and said, "Poor child, at least I don't have to worry about how to find you. I should be paying their ass child support for all of the shit they do for you."

While everybody laughed, Jesse cut in and asked Ra'zee, "Boy, when is that pretty little wife of yours going to get up? I want to see her before you two leave. Plus, I need to go rest. I got a doctor's appointment tomorrow."

Ra'zee looked at Jesse with a snobbish comment on his mind about no one wanting to see all of those tumors in his face. However, before he could speak, Alvona noticed Mei Wei's eye peaking at her from around the corner.

"There she is. Mei Wei, how you feeling baby?" Alvona asked.

Mei Wei dropped her head and covered her face with both hands in embarrassment. Barefoot and still in her husband's personalized Milwaukee Buck's jersey, she trudged through everyone and sat on her husband's lap.

Ra'zee hugged her, smelled her neck and kissed her on the forehead, and then said, "Good morning my little Mugwhy. How are you feeling?"

Mei Wei said nothing as she peaked at him through her hands. Ra'zee knew how she liked to be pampered in the morning, so he adjusted her wedding ring on her hand and kissed her several times all over her hands and face.

Alvona smiled and said, "Mei Wei, did you have fun last night? We sure did."

Mei Wei moved her hands and smiled at Alvona

while she nodded yes several times with child- like eyes. Alvona continued as she raised and twirled her hands in an attempt to mimic Mei Wei's hand gestures. "Girl, I want you to teach me one of those dances you know how to do. I liked that; it was very nice."

Louise sat her bottle down, stood up, and said, "I know how to dance like that too." Then, she started prancing around and pouting her lip like she was exotic and super sexy. Mei Wei couldn't hold her silence any longer and burst out laughing.

Ra'zee tapped her on the thigh and said, "Look out beautiful, I got to go to the bathroom."

When he left, Jesse said, "Mei Wei, it's good to see you and thanks for taking such good care of our baby boy. I can tell that he is very happy because of you."

Mei Wei got up and came around the table, hugged Jesse, and said, "We take care of each other. That's how it should be."

Jesse liked how she looked past the tumors in his face, the regrets between him and Ra'zee, and into his eyes while speaking to him kindly. Then, she shocked him and said, "He may be a little stubborn like his dad, but I know that he always means well."

Jesse looked at Alvona who said, "Thats right, tell him baby. Preach!"

He said, "Are you sure Alvona didn't have you? You two act just alike."

Mei Wei smiled and said, "Ma taught me to be strong and love our family no matter what. Especially at times when they act like they don't deserve it. That's probably when they need it the most."

Before Mei Wei could say another word, Alvona was out of her chair and was squeezing the air out of her with love and affection while yelling, "Thats my girl! That's my girl!"

Jesse smiled as he turned around and walked off. He gathered his jacket and car keys from the coat hook in the hall.

Ra'zee popped out of the bathroom and said, "There's the man that I know all too well. The one with his coat and hat on, leaving. You know what? That's a good look on you."

Jesse solemnly said, "Son, bitterness is an enemy to any relationship. Believe it or not, I still have a lot to offer you. I know you are still angry about the past, and I wish I could change that, but you won't even allow me the chance to atone for my mistakes. Your mother has moved on, I have moved on and you should move on too. You and your wife deserve better. History has been known to repeat itself over time in the form of a generational curse. Sometimes, that curse wears a mask, but still produces the same result. If you don't watch it, it's going to cost you terribly Ra'zee, more than I bet you are willing to pay. Last night, I recognized the game that was brewing between you and your wife. Take this warning from someone who has lived through it. Don't make the same mistake with her that I made with your mom Alvona."

LEGEND OF THE WIDOW MAKER

Ra'zee responded not out of reason, but out of past bitterness, "It is impossible for me to make the same mistakes as you when I am nothing like you."

Jesse smiled at his son's foolishness, and for him to think that he could somehow escape his own genetics. He whipped on his jacket and walked off as he said, "I guess we will see now, won't we there young Decimal."

When he heard Jesse say his nickname, his mind immediately was infused with a series of snapshot images. Images that had taken place over the course of his hustling days in Milwaukee, Wisconsin. Faces of fools that he put in work on since he was the age of fourteen years old. When he first acquired the nickname Decimal. A name given to him by a cutthroat pimp named Double Cross, that he had took a contract from for ten grand to kill a guy that stole twenty thousand dollars from him along with his top prostitute named Asia. It wasn't until after the job was completed that young Decimal found out that the man he had killed was Double Cross's brother and Asia was his wife. Ra'zee shook the memory from his mind like the bitter winter cold that clings to an old leather jacket that's been left in a car all night.

Back in the kitchen, Mei Wei, Alvona, and Uncle Frank sat and talked about Minnesota, her job and summer plans. Alvona hoped that they would come back to visit for the family reunion scheduled on July 9th, 10th, and 11th. Mei Wei hungrily thought about the cold barbeque in the refrigerator and the long ride home.

Alvona smiled and said, "Well, you didn't really eat anything last night. Do you want me to fix you a plate or do you want to take some barbeque for later?"

Mei Wei's dark oceanic blue, almond shaped eyes lit up as her stomach began to growl. Smiling, she asked, "Are there any ribs left?"

Alvona smiled more and said, "How about you eat as much as you want now, and take some for you and that husband of yours for later?"

Mei Wei smiled as she grunted a deep cave woman "Hmm" in excitement, like she was about to hunt for the biggest piece she could find. She dashed to the sink, rinsed off her hands, and literally jumped back down in her chair just as Alvona closed the refrigerator door. Alvona laughed a little as she sat the aluminum foil covered pan on the table in front of wide-eyed Mei Wei.

She said, "My-y-y, someone is hungry."

Mei Wei didn't even look up but wrapped her hair behind her ear and pulled a meaty rib covered in sticky barbeque sauce from the center of the pan. She closed her eyes and mumbled, "Umm" as she took a big bite and wiggled her shoulders back and forth.

Alvona leaned over, kissed Mei Wei on the top of her head, and said, "You go ahead baby."

Her and Uncle Frank went into the living room and sat on the couch. Ra'zee came back around the corner and stood on the side of the kitchen doorway and peeked at his wife. She had barbeque sauce on all fingertips, the tip of her nose, and smeared across her right cheek.

He couldn't help but laugh as he said, "I told you cold barbeque was good after drinking all night."

Mei Wei smiled and said, "This is so good. Do you want some babe?"

Ra'zee smiled as Mei Wei continued to pick piece after piece out of the pan that had lots of sticky sauce on them. Then, he said, "No beautiful, you go ahead and enjoy yourself. I am going outside to smoke a cigarette and to call Juvenile and ask him to check on our house."

Juvenile answered on the second ring, "What up Decimal? What's good with you, you back up top yet?"

Ra'zee said, "Nah big dog, we still at mom's crib. Probably be in traffic in about an hour."

Juvenile replied, "I am on my way to the Stargate for a security meeting. Just hit my line when you get back up top, and I will slide through."

Ra'zee said, "When you get a chance big dog, check on my house for me."

Juvenile laughed and said, "Ain't nobody gonna do nothing to that little dam gingerbread house you and Mei Wei live in. But if I see a bunch of kids running around the neighborhood with swords in karate shoes, I will most definitely let yo ass know."

Ra'zee laughed and said, "Juvenile, if somebody break in my shit with yo big ass around the corner, I am gonna have Mei Wei beat your ass until you find every one of her fans."

"Dam dog, that's what you on? Hold on, I am gonna

make a U-turn. I just rode past your house."

"Ra'zee replied, "Wise choice. I knew you didn't want me to pour no water on that little gremlin about her house."

Once Juvenile got to the house, he said, "Decimal, it looks like someone taped a piece of paper to your front door. Is you getting evicted or did yo wife get selected for jury duty again?"

Ra'zee laughed it off and said, "Nah fool, just grab the letter and read it to me." He listened to the Rich Homie Quan "They Don't Know" CD track that was banging in Juvenile's Yukon. He couldn't help but wonder what the note was about that Juvenile went to get from his door.

When he got back to his truck, he said, "Aye, Decimal. This note is to your girl. It says something about she's supposed to call her mom?"

The phone went silent as Ra'zee looked through the glass door at Mei Wei in the kitchen eating barbeque, and said, "Good looking out big dog. Let me hit you back in a minute."

Juvenile said, "Alright, let me know if you need something. Peace."

Ra'zee said, "Alright, I will let her know Juvee. I appreciate it. Peace." They both hung up.

Ra'zee took a long drag off his Newport and stared at the barren street in front of him. Flashbacks of the day that Mei Wei had called him after she had been kicked out of her home and cut off from her family for him crossed his mind. A day that he had long since tried to forget. Like the noticeable vacancy of her family at their small wedding, neither of them had ever spoken of that day since.

CHAPTER 12
A POND OF NICKELS

T he air in the room was thick with the accent of lavender scented candles and freshly folded laundry. Youa Wei lay still in her bed under the rustled sound of shallow breaths. The raphe part of her brain slowly released high levels of serotonin that pushed her deeper and deeper into a REM state of sleep. Faint beams of light cascaded through an array of broken blinds that were pulled tightly shut in the room. Every couple of minutes, Youa Wei's eyelids flickered as her mind sifted through the images and sounds that it both collected and weighed through a process of elimination. Once her mind finally settled on a series of comfortable images, it ran a loop of high-definition enhanced video footage and formulated a passageway for her into an alternate reality.

The place she appeared at was located by the entry way of Webber Park, just southwest of Ridgedale Mall. The temperature in the park was pleasant. The landscaped scenery itself was opulent. It displayed requisite beauty along with vibrant water pool activities. Youa Wei quietly strolled toward a vacant park bench positioned opposite a mixed bed of budded dandelions, flowers, and red berry bushes. Shortly after she sat down, she noticed a decrepit tree that shielded a small pond from public sight. The tree bore a strange, pomegranate like fruit that hung from chalk like stems on a couple of branches. Each piece of fruit whispered secrets of knowledge in Aramaic to a dark figure dressed in all white that stood upon the water. A large, black mamba snake coiled as it moved in and out of the clusters of fruit that hung like hives from the middle of the branches. The left side of the tree was sunk deep into the ground. Blood washed lily pads spotted with highly polished nickels floated in the sediment filled pond. The figure in the midst of the pond wore all white from head to toe. His fedora style brim exposed cranial bone along with seared skin across his neck. His muscular back beyond the wife beater t-shirt revealed charred skin as if struck by a passing bolt of lightning. Re-bonded to the bone, horribly contorted living dead muscle tissue covered his left shoulder and right arm. His creased dress pants were blood dipped at the one-inch cufflink across the hard sole bottomed dress shoes that he wore.

She walked closer just as he flung his white dress shirt across the dead rooted side of the tree, like at the edge of a work bench in a shop. Then, he walked over and reached beneath an old bramble bush. The bush shook as he grabbed hold of the foot of a woman and pulled her into the pond. Mei Wei swung her arms wildly and clawed at the loose soil as she struggled to break loose from the powerful grip of the figure that dragged her with ease onto the blood washed water that was covered in lily pads spotted by nickels.

The Widow Maker turned toward Youa Wei as she stood up and screamed, "Daughter!"

A sadistic grin spread across the right side of his jawline absent of pieces of flesh. He reached for six blood covered nickels from a lily pad that floated by, then jammed three into each one of Mei Wei's eye sockets right through her oceanic blue pupils. He held his head back in ecstasy as he forced her head beneath the waters and shivered over the gurgle of her water choked screams and said, "Stop your squirming, the Light of Death is upon you!"

Youa Wei kicked and screamed in bed as she fought her way off from under the freshly folded laundry that she had buried herself under in her sleep. Xiao Lee almost knocked the bedroom door off from its hinges as he burst into the room to sounds of screams from his wife. Laundry continued to fly while Youa Wei screamed amid shorts gasps for air and swung wildly as though she was being drowned.

Xiao Lee blocked several kicks until he made his way past her defenses and yelled, "Youa! Wake up!"

He then shook her awake. When she came through, terror and huge tear drops filled her eyes. The familiar face of her husband came into focus, and she immediately sought to use him as shield. In his protective embrace, she balled up his shirt in her small hand. Then, she looked around the room to make certain that her attacker had not followed her there and that she was safe. Her nerves took a few minutes to settle. Xiao Lee assured her that she was safe until she closed her eyes and sighed in relief.

When her thoughts cleared, he said, "I have never seen you like that. I thought that someone had broken into the house and was trying to kill you. Can you recall what happened in your dream?"

Youa Wei looked down at her white knuckled grip; she still had her husband's shirt balled up in her hand. Slowly, she let go, flattened his shirt against his chest, and wiped the tears from her eyes. Slowly, she exhaled in exhaustion, then scooted to the top of the bed by the headboard as she pulled her knees into her chest. Xiao Lee watched her momentarily, then looked around the room at the laundry that was scattered across the dressers and the floor. when he looked back at Youa Wei, their eyes briefly met. Then, she slowly turned her attention and quietly stared outside at the wind-whipped snow drift that came past the side of the blinds that covered the window.

After several minutes of silence, Youa Wei spoke although her eyes never left the barren tree in their backyard. "Um, um.." she grunted softly to clear her throat. "It all seemed so real, like I was really there."

Xiao Lee listened carefully as Youa Wei told him about the few pieces she could remember about her dream. In mid speech while she described the decrepit tree, the blood-filled pond, the horrible figure dressed in all white, and the brutal slaying that she witnessed, she suddenly whipped her head towards him as she remembered the woman being killed was her daughter Mei Wei.

Xiao Lee said nothing until she was completely done, and then he asked, "Do you think this dream is a reflection of some of the fears that you have about what Mei Wei has been doing and the life that she lives now?"

Panic and urgency seized her mind as huge tear drops formed on her eyelashes. She struggled at first while she fanned her tears. Then she broke beyond her loss of ability and said, "No, no something is wrong. I can feel it!"

Xiao Lee stood up and walked over to the other side of the bed and held his wife's hand as he said, "Youa Wei, listen to me. I know that when you get worked up about something, you don't like to ease into it. Instead, you usually plow right into it without any hesitation. Now, I am not saying that you are wrong. I am asking how do you think Mei Wei is going to take it? If the first thing you ask her, when you see her is "Daughter, what kind of life have you been living? I had this horrible dream that you were being killed by some dark figure dressed in all white." You do remember that Mei Wei never practiced any of the mystic arts. She instead always wanted to go hang out with her Christian church going friends. I remember her coming back and asking us about the teachings of the Bible and if we had ever heard of their teacher Yeshua Ha' Maschiach called Jesus Christ. More than likely, she is going to think you are mad and that you contacted her out of religious belief, not to reconcile our family. Please, just think about the best way to share this with her before you do. For I know that you won't let this go, right?"

Youa Wei wiped her tears and smiled politely in respect to her husband's wisdom. Then she laughed a little and said, "So you think I just plow through things. Husband, you make me sound so passionate."

Xiao Lee laughed and said, "Passionate? More like stubborn and moody."

Youa Wei laughed and hit her husband with a pillow from the bed. Then, she looked around the room at the mess and said, "Wow, this room looks like a tornado hit it. I should clean this up and then come downstairs and fix you some tea."

Xiao Lee smiled as he patted his wife on the leg and said, "Here, I will help you pick up our things. Never mind making tea. How about we go to the mall for a while and get a few items for the house. It will do some good in helping to clear your mind?" Like all women regardless of culture, Youa Wei loved to shop.

Smiling, she said, "If I had known me having a nightmare would end up in us going shopping, I would have had one much sooner."

Xiao Lee laughed as he leaned in and kissed his wife

on the forehead and said, "Now that sounds like a nightmare to me."

While they picked up and refolded the laundry that was scattered around the room, Youa Wei wondered if her daughter was truly okay. Even more so, if she would take the dark warning that she believed came from her ancestors to save Mei Wei.

Ra'zee stared at Mei Wei and wondered what the best way was to tell her about the note from her mom that Juvenile got off the door at the house. Seeing her so happy made him feel even more reluctant to say anything until they got home. He knew that she would be upset at the news, but pissed off at him, especially once she learned that he knew about the note from her mom and said nothing. He decided that his best course of action was to just simply tell her so that she would be prepared. Also, so that they would have support from his mom if she took it extremely hard.

When Ra'zee came into the kitchen, Mei Wei's eyes were still dead locked on the pan of barbeque. She asked in between bites, "Are you sure you don't want any now?"

Ra'zee responded in a low tone, "No beautiful, I am okay."

Mei Wei cut her eyes at him. She could tell by the sound of his voice that something was bothering him. She immediately lost her appetite in apprehension of what it was and stood up from the table to wash her hands.

Ra'zee wasted no time, cleared his throat, and said, "There is no easy way to say this, so I am just going to say it. I just got off the phone with Juvenile. I asked him to swing by and check on our house. He said that there was a note on the front door," he paused briefly then said, "for you to call your mom."

Mei Wei dismissed the report as nothing and continued to wash her hands in silence. Then, she mumbled to herself, "I don't even know what she wants with me. We have spoken in almost five years."

Ra'zee said nothing but stood there by her side in silence. Suddenly, she slapped the water off, pushed past him and said, "Move babe, I have to go pee."

After Ra'zee heard the bathroom door close, he followed behind her and waited in the hall. Alvona tip toed to the coat hook and asked, "Is everything okay?"

Ra'zee forced a faint smile toward his mom and said, "She will be fine. I just got word that there was a note on the door at our house from her mom."

Alvona gasped as she covered her mouth. Then she said, "Poor baby! How long has it been, almost five years?"

Ra'zee nodded in agreement with his mom's calculated timetable. Alvona finished with, "I raised you to be a good man. You stay right here until she feels like talking, okay?" and walked off.

Ra'zee said, "Don't worry mom, I will." Then he sat on the floor against the bathroom door and listened quietly to his wife cry. About twenty minutes later, when he finally heard the knob on the bathroom door twist, he stood up and stretched. Mei Wei opened the door, and he could tell that she had relived the pain of that night. He held her tight as she wept bitterly on his chest.

After several minutes, she looked up at him and he softly asked, "Do you want to go home now?"

Through puffy eyes and sniffles, she nodded yes as the tears continued to fall. Ra'zee led her by the hand into the bedroom and packed their things while she slowly dressed zombified. As if frozen in time, she watched as a huge tear drop like a snow globe fell from her eye to the floor. In it were little glass figurines that depicted the violent scene of the night she told Xiao Lee and her mom about her plans to marry Ra'zee. She trembled when the image hit the floor, exploded like dust, and was carried away by the wind.

CHAPTER 13
LOVE LIES

⊸◦C⌇◦⊷

The ride back to Maplewood was mostly quiet. Mei Wei wondered what her mother would say when they actually talked. Ra'zee, on the other hand, didn't care what the hell she wanted. In his eyes, she was an intruder and about to fuck everything up. He had finally gotten his wife's attitude to where he wanted it to be. Now, her mother that had abandoned her sought to undo that. With her very presence, she could resuscitate the old, boring, rigid, super square wife that he had grown tired of. There was no way that he would ever allow that. Mei Wei belonged to him, and he wasn't about to let anyone, not even Youa Wei, change that. It wasn't long before his thoughts consumed him, and he asked Mei Wei if she wanted to make a quick stop with him to get a drink to calm their nerves. It didn't take much mental coaching on his part. For if she had learned anything about liquor, it was that it was good at helping her forget her pain.

Mei Wei said, "You have no idea how much I want a drink right now. I never thought I would hear from my mom again. Right now, I don't have a clue what I am going to say to her or what she is going to tell me after all this time. Knowing her, it's probably all bad news that she wants to tell me anyways."

Ra'zee just listened as she vented. Mei Wei continued, "Babe, I'm not even dressed appropriately to be in public. I mean, wearing shorts and your basketball jersey in this weather is me basically wearing pajamas."

Ra'zee smiled and said in a comforting voice, "Do not worry beautiful. I know the perfect store we can stop at. I am sure you'll find something there that you like. Then, we can go stop for drinks for a little bit, okay?"

Mei Wei said, "Shopping and liquor? I think that I am going to like hanging out with you Decimal." Then she giggled.

Ra'zee laughed and said, "Oh yeah? Next, you'll be talking about you wanting to hustle."

Mei Wei responded in her bad girl voice, "Babe, I have hustled before."

Ra'zee said, "Oh yeah? Doing what?"

Mei Wei lowered her head and grew quiet. Ra'zee said, "Beautiful, you can tell me anything."

Mei Wei looked out the window and said, "If I tell

you, you will look at me differently and I like how you look at me with innocent eyes. Truth is, I am not the good girl that you think I am."

Ra'zee replied, "There is nothing that can change how I feel about you. You are my wife and I love you. So just tell me."

Mei Wei looked at him while he was checking the side mirrors and switching lanes. Then, she softly said, "Before my mom and dad split, he was very abusive. One day, he hit my mom, and I tried to kill him with a butcher knife. I remember I came in the house after I heard him slap her. I whispered to him to calm down, and that it was okay. Then I hugged him as I leaned around him and grabbed the butcher knife from the box on the counter. Then, I held on to him for dear life as I stabbed him over and over again. I was a first-time offense juvenile, so I got probation."

Ra'zee responded unmercifully, "He had that shit coming. He better be glad that you didn't kill his ass."

Mei Wei smiled and said, "Another time, me and some kids in high school robbed this drunk man wo was trying to hit on me with a lot of money."

Ra'zee commented instantly, "He shouldn't have been flashing it."

Mei Wei asked playfully, "Can I do any wrong in your eyes?"

Ra'zee responded in a serious tone, "Nope. I do not care what the situation is. They say two wrongs don't make a right, but I damn sure believe in making it even."

When they reached Madison, Wisconsin, they stopped off at a specialty store off Monroe Avenue named Razzmatazz. This store was known to carry stylish garments suitable for any occasion. Ra'zee picked out a casual Gucci shirt and pants with Rockport shoes. Mei Wei found a very nice candy apple red, long spaghetti strap shoulder blouse, black fitted skinny jeans, and Stacy Miller flats that were burgundy with red bottoms.

When she came out of the dressing room, Ra'zee said, "Damn, you look good! I don't think that I have ever seen you dress like that."

Mei Wei blushed and said, "I always wanted to, but never had a reason to. Plus, I didn't know how you would react, because I thought that you wanted a square wife. I mean, ain't that what attracted you to me in the record shop?"

Ra'zee laughed and said, "That was part of it, just like you were attracted to the hustler in me. Now, it makes even more sense because you definitely got a little hustler in you. Still, I like that you are a good girl that I can trust. The one that I can call at 3 am and know exactly where you are at. I must admit that I am kind of feeling this whole you being Bonnie to my Clyde. Back in the day, me and you would have made a formidable alliance in the game amongst other things."

Then, he leaned in and kissed her. Mei Wei's mind told her that she was about to cross the line but did it anyway. Curiosity led her through her need to prove herself. Her heart picked up in pace as her knees felt weak.

"I wouldn't mind making a little money on the side with you. As long as it's not too dangerous. I mean, I wouldn't want anything to happen to you."

Ra'zee said, "We'll see, because I definitely don't want to put you in any harm's way."

Mei Wei smiled and said, "I know you'd watch out for me." Then she went and changed back into her clothes before she headed to the checkout counter. Ra'zee let his mind drift for a minute. He recalled many of the low grade hustles he had done once. He had worked in auto mechanic chop shops, sold hot electronics and even re-rocked dope (crack cocaine blown up with 7up soda to quadruple the size although it diminishes the potency).

Old desires stirred in him to be like his predecessor in the game, Double Cross. He had three bad bitches that he sent out of state on the regular of which he sicced on the unexpected hood rich. Their physical beauty, sexual appetite, ability to bond with all kids in their boyfriend's family, and especially their momma with a warm protective rage made them extremely difficult to resist. With that skill set, it didn't take long for them to graduate from girlfriend to wifey status, gain access to a couple of money moves, and learn where the main safe was at. Once the chess board was set and all of the pawns were in place, they would call Double Cross who would send Asia. She was the deadliest: 5'2", 125 lb. Korean and African American prostitute that he had in his arsenal. Her signature move after robbing someone with a lot of dirt was to burn the place down. Whoever it belonged to tried to get as far away as they could from the incident to avoid being at the center of a police investigation. Once, these two girls got together and went out for a lady's night. All of the information would be verified third party to Double Cross with a time window to hit the location of the safe. This game of love lies yielded Double Cross about $80,000 a month in jewelry, drugs, weapons, and cash.

Ra'zee smiled while he watched Mei Wei at the checkout counter. Then, he pictured himself sending Mei Wei to collect information the same way Asia was sent by Double Cross. From then on, he set it in his heart to test the waters to see if Mei Wei could in fact handle that level of the game, or if she was just all talk.

The bar that Ra'zee chose was located off the west side of Madison just off of I-94 on Allied Drive. It was spotted with only a few customers that were locals who were enjoying the football game on the big screen. Before they went inside, Ra'zee told Mei Wei, "Alright, let's get some ground rules before we go in here, because this is a first for you and I."

Mei Wei looked curious at him and asked, "What did you have in mind?"

Ra'zee cleared his throat and said, "First of all, this is still my old backyard and there is no telling what or who we might run across. So, pay attention to everyone and everything. Secondly, you need a nickname that you are comfortable with. Never use your real name in public, just in case something goes sideways. This will keep people out of your personal life and protect our home."

Mei Wei's eyes lit up and she started clapping as if she was part of the cast for some upcoming play. She said, "So I get to call you Decimal all the time."

Decimal laughed and said, "Just in traffic. And what should I call you..."

Mei Wei cut him off and said, "My old middle school nickname from when I was a bad ass, Jade."

Decimal looked at her seriously and said, "Jade huh? Okay, Jade it is. I am feeling that."

Jade said, "We are still married though, so don't have me beat some girl's ass about you."

Decimal thought about the hustle and said, "You set the limits. The only limit I am setting is you must watch how fast you drink. Do not allow any liquor to take your mental balance and you end up about to snap like you did with Jenny."

Jade laughed and said, "Oh, I went there and had you not gotten in the way, I was about to stomp her ass out in that hallway."

Decimal sternly said, "I know it, but what you have to know is that there is a time and a season for everything under the sun. There will be opportunities to settle scores and make money. You have to, we have to, make sure that we do not jeopardize what we have in the process of making money moves or putting a stamp on someone who crossed that line."

Jade said, "This is more of your world than mine. So, I will just follow your lead. Just say something like Gremlin to if something is up or Mugwhy if it's all good. That way, I will know what I should be doing, okay babe?"

Decimal nodded and said, "Do not worry, I got you. Come on, let's go inside. Hopefully, its quiet in here and we can just chill for about an hour, two tops, and then get back on the road. They used to have good fried fish in here too. If you eat while you are drinking, it will help you to keep your balance. And if you are going to drink, you are going to have to figure out what works best for you. A drunk in public don't do nothing but draw a lot of unnecessary attention." Jade hung her head in embarrassment as Decimal finished with, "But that don't mean you can't have some serious fun."

Then, he twirled her around and said, "Damn, you look sexy. I just know one of these old fools is going to offer you his social security check."

Jade smiled and strutted off in front of Decimal as she said, "We got a few bills that they can pay on the regular. I am sure with a little thought; I can think up a few more."

Decimal said, "Jade, Jade, Jade," as he pulled open the door.

Several pair of eyes locked on them when they stepped into the bar. A retired man wearing clean dress slacks, a crisp white dress shirt, and several gold rings winked at Jade instantly. Decimal saw it, but ignored it and nodded to the bartender instead, who smiled as he recognized him instantly.

"Mac, what's going down old school. I see you still holding it down," said Decimal with a mob boss smile on his face.

Mac made his way from behind the bar as he spread his arms in respect to embrace his friend and said, "Dammit Decimal, boy where the hell you been? I ain't seen your ass in thirty damn Sundays! Show me some love. And who is this fine young thing with you?"

Decimal gave Mac a hug and turned to introduce Mei Wei. As soon as he said, "I am good. Figured I would slide down on you since I was down in Milwaukee with Mei..."

Mei Wei nudged Decimal in the side while she smiled at Mac and announced, "Hi! I am Jade." Then, she looked up at decimal and said, "I am going to go to the bathroom. Will you get me a drink?"

Decimal said, "Absolutely," as Mac went back behind the counter. When she passed the man sitting at the middle of the bar, he watched every step that she took and traced every curve of her body.

Jade politely said, "Hi, how are you today?"

He replied softly, "A whole lot better now that I have seen you."

Jade smiled and kept walking. Secretly, she liked how he complimented her and spoke low to not draw any attention to not disrespect Decimal. In the bathroom, she whispered to herself, "This is my chance to prove to Decimal that I can handle the game."

CHAPTER 14
FOOTSTEPS IN THE DARK

———⇒∘⟨⟩∘⇐———

The suburban neighborhood looked bleak underneath the winter storm's threat. To keep her from driving back alone, Misty decided to drop McIntyre off at home out in Rosemont, Minnesota on Coleshire Path. When they got out of the car, McIntyre quickly wrapped her face to try to desensitize her receptors that were acutely heightened from crying most of the afternoon at the hospital. An unforeseen phone call from Maria, her daughter in law, had refreshed traumatic memories of the nightmare that surrounded her only child Carlos. Subsequently, the news of Carlos' struggles triggered an emotional breakdown unlike anything she had experienced in years. It had almost been three years since she thought about the nightmare. A nightmare filled with terror-stricken nights behind her locked bedroom door, under the covers in bed. Horrific news reports on national news channels like CNN and Carlos' flight into the bayous. A nightmare that her mind, in its struggle to survive, had set up many psychological barriers to black out the faintest memories of the most difficult time in her life. She even went to the extreme and took down every photo of Carlos in the house and acted as if he never even existed.

Initially, Misty was amazed that in a matter of moments, one phone call had exposed all of McIntyre's self-deception and uncovered many secrets buried in her heart. Thirteen hours later, she stood in the driveway a mere shell of the woman that had walked out of the same house earlier that morning. The sun blinded her eyes. The wind cut sharply into her nose. Her head pounded fiercely from heightened senses. It was so quiet on Coleshire Path that the crunch of the snow, as she stepped on each lightly dust covered step, that the sound echoed in her ears as if through a bull horn. This caused her to feel disoriented. Once inside the house, she quickly changed into loose pajama pants, a t-shirt titled, "Pre- med", and discarded her socks. She settled into a comfortable chair in her living room in front of Misty and took several deep breaths. Misty waited quietly as McIntyre gathered her thoughts and began from the beginning.

A solitary tear fell from her right eye as she stared out of the bay window that overlooked the front yard and said, "Three years ago, I lied to you when I told you that Carlos had decided to go away to college out of state. Truth is, he left for a totally different reason."

McIntyre whipped her head towards Misty as tears streamed down her face. With a quiver on her lips and a crackle in her voice, McIntyre begged, "Misty, promise me you will not tell anyone of this. They won't understand."

Misty moved forward to the edge of the sofa. She had never seen McIntyre like this. She asked, "Are you and Carlos in some kind of danger?"

McIntyre continues, distracted by her own thoughts as if she had not even heard Misty's questions. "They won't believe me. Besides, if he finds out I told you, he might come for me... and for you."

"Carmen, you're scaring me. Who is this person you are talking about that has you so afraid?"

Carmen grew very quiet as she looked at Mistry through the disheveled mess of long hair that covered her face. Misty thought to herself, "She looks like she's experiencing a psychotic break."

With a sweat drenched face as she looked over her shoulder at the darkened staircase leading to the upstairs, McIntyre said, "No, no. On second thought, I have told you too much already. He knows things. Dark secrets of such things that some try to hide. He cannot be bargained with, reasoned with, or bought off. It's probably already too late. He could be here right now: waiting, watching, listening. I should be quiet."

Misty stood up as she asked Carmen, "Is there someone else in the house Carmen?"

She said nothing as she began to rock back and forth while slowly whispering "Lux Ab Exitium Velle Venre" over and over again. Misty cautiously made her way to the steps while her gaze stayed fixated on the darkness at the tops of the stairs. McIntyre's voice slowly rose in the backdrop as the floorboards creaked behind Misty's ascension of the staircase. With the weight of her body on the third step and her right foot raised toward the fourth, she froze in mid step. Panic seized her mind and heart rapidly picked up pace. For she heard what sounded like hard sole dress shoes walking towards the top of the stairs. She turned to run and found McIntyre standing right in front of her.

In her proud, motherly voice, she said, "Misty, won't you stay for dinner? My Carlos will be home soon."

With the sound of the footsteps now descending the stairs, Misty ran out of the side entrance door and to her car. Inside, she fumbled for her car keys and dropped them several times onto the floor. Once she finally got the car started, she looked back at the house and noticed McIntyre standing in the driveway with her bare feet in the snow and ice. The car fishtailed until it found traction through the snow and out of the driveway. As she gained speed, Misty looked in her rearview mirror and saw Carmen turn her head as if summoned and walk back up the driveway to the house. She went back into the house as she said a prayer for strength.

Just after she had closed her eyes with her back on the door, she sensed another pair of eyes that stared at her. Then, the sound of hard sole dress shoes approached from the living room. Startled, she opened her eyes and saw Dr. Marcus Rutowski walking towards her.

With a warm smile, he said, "I hope you don't mind. I found your front door open and after calling your name several times to no avail, I decided to let myself in."

McIntyre raised her hand in dismissal of the intrusion. Dr. Rutowski was not only her old psychology professor, but he was also her son's psychiatrist. Long before she attempted to smile, his specialized training in observational behavior had already begun to profile her. He did this in the same way he would a typical client on his specialized and unique caseload. In one swift glance, he carefully observed that the pupils of her eyes were extraordinarily dilated. Additionally, her physical posture appeared to be weakened as if she would collapse at any moment. Her thin "pre-med" t-shirt was completely soaked at the collar with droplets of water marks on her shoulder. This indicated to him that she had recently splashed handfuls of water on her face in an attempt to emotionally decompress.

Further observation led him to notice that she had on pajama pants, which was highly unusual for a resident nurse trainer at this hour of the day. It was more realistic to find her still in hospital scrubs. Finally, when his glance reached the floor, he noticed the crushed ice on her three smallest toes and a puddle of water beneath her bare feet. A strong and clear indication that she had been outside barefoot in the snow. He quickly assessed that whatever had triggered this emotional disarrangement had to been provoked by some event at work, but by what is what intrigued him. He rationalized that this was very unlike RNT McIntrye, his most prized student. He had used her in several speaking engagements at the U of M, Minneapolis campus. She also was spoken of very highly at the hospital and had always displayed great personal strength. There was only one weakness he had known her to have. A universal kink that had the ability to affect any mother's armor. Hers being her only child, Carlos.

Dr. Rutowski said nothing as he gazed upon her with his usual truth absorbent smile. His rare ability to look beyond the visage that many tried to carry made him the perfect substitute vessel for the Light of Death himself, the Widow Maker. McIntyre tried to portray a warm, hospitable attitude. Although, deep inside her soul cringed under the excruciating pain of her heartache for Carlos.

Curiosity struck her as to why Dr. Rutowski would come by in the middle of a snowstorm. With a purely exterior smile, she said, "It is good to see you Dr. Rutowski. Were you just in the area and decided to stop by or is there something else in specific you wanted to discuss?"

Dr. Rutowski thought to himself, "This can't be just a mere coincidence between what I experienced two days ago at St. Peters psychiatric hospital. Within the departure of the Widow Maker and Carmen's appearance today. She must know something. I must find him. There's so much more I have to learn. I must discover the secrets of his origin."

With the smile of a skilled interviewer, he asked, "Do you mind if we sit and chat for a brief moment? I would like to speak to you about your son, young Carlos."

McIntyre's eyes slightly flickered at the mention of Carlos' name, and Dr. Rutowski knew that he had touched the source of her recent trauma. Once Carmen was seated in her favorite chair, Dr. Rutowski chose a corner seat of the sofa and leaned slightly back to conceal his face by the shadow in the room. A personal interviewing habit of his that reflected his desire to have one not focus on his presences, but purely his voice.

"Do you have something you wish to share with me?"

McIntyre followed his prompt by lowering her head in distress and saying, "I am glad you stopped by. As you can tell, I have had a very tough day and could use your counsel."

Dr. Rutowski's voice was low, intuitive as he searchingly said, "Carmen, you know that you can confide in me about anything. Please tell me more. First, I would like to know if this is a work-related issue you need to sort through or if it's more of a personal matter to find closure with?"

She responded with uncertainty, "Maybe it's a little

of both? This morning when I got out of bed, I felt an unusual chill in the house. I dismissed it as nothing more than an odd fluctuation in the weather which has been the normal lately."

From out of the shadows, his low calculated response whispered, "Weather anomalies do appear to be the new norm. Then what happened?"

She took a deep breath and continued, "Well, I grabbed a sweatshirt on my way to adjust the heat in the hall. There, I was met by this god-awful stench that came from Carlos' room. It smelled like blood and dead rodents." Dr. Rutowski leaned forward upon hearing the description of the scent. Only his face broke the plane of darkness that concealed it by a shadow.

"I covered my nose and went to open a window in there. When I reached for the doorknob, I could have sworn I saw a shadow move across the floor through the light that came from underneath the door. When I opened it, the scent was gone, and no one was there." Dr. Rutowski's face slowly receded back into the darkness as he reclined again into the sofa. He closed his eyes and continued to listen as his thoughts drifted towards the Widow Maker. Carmen's voice grew faint in his hearing and had almost completely dissipated until he heard, "Then out of the blue, I received a phone call at the hospital from Maria about Carlos being in some kind of trouble. His recent behaviors have been quite disturbing."

His eyes instantly widened in the darkness at the

name of Carlos' name. Cleverly, he tossed a mental wedge into the cracked doorway of her mind that led to secrets he sought to uncover. He asked, "Who is this, Maria?"

McIntyre responded without much thought, "She is Carlos' fiancé."

He slightly kicked the mental wedge to open the door further, "Did she indicate where they were or perhaps them coming by?"

Frustrated, she yelled, "That the problem. I blacked out. I completely lost it. I started hyperventilating and crying again. My friend Misty had to bring me home from work."

Dr. Rutowski stood and walked over to the bay window and looked outside as he said, "Carmen, if I am to truly help Carlos overcome this severe psychosis that he is gripped by, which I fear that if his delusion sets in again will be permanent, you must tell me where to find him."

McIntyre responded, "All I know is that they are somewhere in the Louisiana bayous."

PART 3: THE HOURGLASS OF BONES

CHAPTER 15
THE MOTEL OF REGRET

———————⟡⟡⟡———————

The worn piece of gray duct tape flapped repeatedly as it hung loosely from the broken blade inside of the dingy white plastic box fan. With each rotation of the wheel, the tape rapped lightly against the screen cover like impatient fingers ticking down time towards an impending engagement. Only three of its original four blades were left on the fan wheel which caused it to wobble rapidly on high speed and nearly tip over several times. Slowly, Carlos' mind drifted behind the sound of the synchronized hits of the flap in the fan. Oddly enough, it reminded him of the sound that his hand fashioned version of the Roman cat-o-nine-tails made when laid upon human flesh. The shrewd contraption of a medieval braided cord with jagged pieces of glass and nails in it was the chosen instrument of the Widow Maker. He had used this device to teach penance and therefore subsequently had scourged many of his victims with it. The sound grew until it consumed the large humid and sticky family room.

Meanwhile, Maria laid cuddled with Jaysiah half asleep on the adjacent couch in front of a fuzzy picture of an old western movie on TV. The faint laughter of the girls, Rita and Katherine, who giggled at nap time, whispered from down the hall. Carlos eased off the couch and headed towards the condemned attic space to meditate. He desperately needed further counsel of the Dark One as to what to do about Ms. Hatchfield's body. The body that he had contorted in the heavy trunk that was now buried in the old family cemetery at Stonewall Plantation. When Carlos stepped into the attic, he instantly felt the comfort of the darkness and longed for the old toolshed behind his mother's house up in Rosemont, Minnesota. It wasn't soon after his soul embraced the decadent darkness that he had begun to hear the familiar chime of six nickels falling to the ground as his vision grew hazy.

The latch to the attic door clicked shut and Maria turned over in her sleep only to notice that he was gone. A chill swept over her flesh as she looked at Jaysaiah and whispered, "Where has your father gone this time? I wish your grandmother were here."

Maria closed her eyes and held on tightly to Jaysiah as she began to cry. Secretly, she knew what was happening again and wondered if their little family would survive the darkness. The darkness that she knew had returned to consume Carlos yet again.

Decimal watched the playful eyes between Jade and the older gentleman at the opposite end of the bar. He knew that she had caught his eye as soon as they entered the bar. Jade speculated that if Decimal wasn't there, she would've had all those crisp $100 bills in his pockets by now. Bills he had no problem flashing to try to get her attention.

With a grand smile, Mac asked, "Decimal, you want me to top off you and your lady friend's drink? No charge of course."

Decimal said, "Sure Man. Then I hate to have to tell you this, but we need to take off. We still have about four house to go before we get back up top."

Mac laughed lightly and said, "Come on Decimal. There you go with that again. It'll probably be another six months before I see you again and the party just got started."

Decimal replied, "Me and Jade are going to start making it our habit to shoot by mom's out by the airport in Milwaukee. I will slide through when we come back this way for the family reunion in mid-July."

Jade finished the Boone's Farm wine in her glass, ate two more of the potato wedges in her lunch basket then said, "Well, sounds like that's my cue. I got to go to the bathroom. Then I will be ready to go."

Decimal replied to her, "I'm going to go start the car

so it can warm up. Mac, it's been a pleasure. Mugwhy, I will be outside so don't take all day."

When Jade heard the key word Mugwhy, she smiled knowing that Decimal had given her the green light to get that money. She grabbed her purse and a napkin and headed to the bathroom. She held the gaze of the man at the end of the bar until she got close to the bathroom. As soon as she passed him, she baited him and said, "That drink looks really good. I hope you enjoy it and the rest of your day."

The man looking for a window of opportunity quickly responded, "It would be even better if you had one with me."

Jade dropped the napkin by his feet, then quickly stooped to pick it up and handed it to him underneath the bar with her eyeliner pencil. "You should write your number down so I can call you for a drink the next time I'm down this way."

The man said, "Sure thing, but I don't stay down this was. I actually stay up in Eau Claire. You ever been up that way?"

Jade was about to mention living in Maplewood until she remembered what Ra'zee said about protecting their home. She stumbled over her words as she said, "I stay in Maple... I mean, we may be able to have drinks closer up north then. I stay in Minneapolis."

He said, "Show me the purple baby. I like Minnesota. I'm Leonard, but my friends call me Leo for short like the zodiac."

Jade's eyes sparkled as she said, "I'm Ja..."

He cut back in and said, "Jade, I know, I was listening. A little skill set I picked up on in the military for recalling small details in my surroundings. Hell, with a detail as fine as you, I don't see myself forgetting you anytime soon."

Jade then asked, "Will you excuse me? I have to use the bathroom before we go. I will get your number on the way out."

Leo studied every curve of Jade's legs as she went on to the bathroom and said, "Hey, I got my good eye on you. You let me know if you need any help in there?"

He quickly wrote his cellphone number down on the napkin. When she came out, he handed it to her inside a fifty-dollar bill, and said, "Will you please play a song for me in the jukebox on your way out? I like a variety of music." Jade smiled when she saw the crisp fifty-dollar-bill. She looked back over her shoulder and said, "I just knew that I was going to like you."

Leo replied, "Oh, it's greater later baby!"

Happy about the fifty dollars, but not sure what to play, she punched in the first song by the Isley Brothers she saw. It just so happened to be that the song was a classic and a favorite jam for the both of them. "Caravan of Love" shook the old speaker system with style and grace. The music sounded so beautiful that not even old Mac could resist the urge to do the two-step as he slid from behind the bar. Jade figured she had done both of them justice from seeing both happy and reminiscing like old timers do.

She heard Leo tell Mac over the music, "Boy, you don't know nothing about this here. See, that there is the Isley Brothers. You was still wet behind the ears when this came out."

Mac responded, "Young, dumb, full of cum and getting all of the ladies sprung. I remember back in the day this girl named Loretta!" She laughed and figured why ruin such a good thing, so she punched in every Isley Brother's song she could find and quickly left the bar. Her smile slowly left her face when she saw Ra'zee standing on the curb pissed off next to the spot where their car was stolen from.

"Dammit, I should have known to put all of those shopping bags in the trunk. Especially in this crack infested neighborhood! Whoever stole our car probably think they hit the jackpot, "he yelled.

Mei Wei asked, "what are we going to do babe?"

Ra'zee said, "I called Juvenile and asked him to come get us. It will take a minute, but he will be here."

Mei Wei quickly said, "Well I have an idea if you're up for it?"

Ra'zee smiled and said, "I'm all ears."

Mei Wei looked at the ground and said, "That one old guy in there that was hitting on me. His name is Leonard, Leo for short. He stays up in Eau Claire. I am sure I could get him to drop us off in Minneapolis since he already gave me fifty dollars to play some music on the jukebox for him. I would probably have to sit next to him and have like two drinks first?"

Decimal smiled at her, as he thought about Double Cross and Asia. Then he said, "Well, Jade, if you think you can handle it? Otherwise, we can wait on Juvee?"

Jade said, "I got this. Leo just wants some attention and someone to tell his stories to."

Decimal said, "I will be watching, let's go." Then he called Juvenile and told him he secured a ride to back up top but would still need him to pick them up in Minneapolis. When they came back in the door, Mac smiled at Decimal and Leo smiled at Jade. Decimal then said, "Change of plans Mac. We are going to hang out for a little bit."

Mac watched Jade as she went and sat by Leo. Then, he looked at Decimal, gave his nod of approval, and said, "My man, play on playa. Let me get you a drink."

Leo yelled from the other end, "Mac, let me get another drink and get Ms. Jade anything she wants."

Mac obliged and after several drinks over only five songs, Jade quickly saw that Leo drank like a fish and would probably be there until close. So, she faked a call to her cousin and disappointment of no ride coming to get them. Leo quickly offered them a ride toward Eau Claire with him. At Decimal's prompt, Jade suggested to Leo that he not drink too much more. That way, they could make the ride before it got too late. Leo agreed with a counteroffer that jade have one last drink with him in Eau Claire before he dropped them off. Quiet confidence grew in Jade, and she knew just the way that she could get the rest of his money with very little effort.

Although the inside of the 2018 MKX was luxurious, the ride to Eau Claire was uncomfortable for Mei Wei. While she wondered what her husband was thinking, who eyed her in the sideview passenger mirror from the backseat. Leo held her hand and whispered some of the strangest flirtations to her that she had ever heard.

With a grin on his face, he lifted her hand, licked her wedding ring, nibbled on her pinky finger, and said, "Gobble, gobble, you know I was breast fed as a baby?" she giggled as he continued, "You look so good right now, I would drink your dirty bathwater. I bet you have pretty feet, don't you?"

Decimal laughed and asked, "What kind of music do you got in here old school?"

Leo said, "Not too much that you would be into youngster."

"Oh yeah, try me," Decimal said.

Annoyed by Decimal's repeated interruptions, Leo slyly said, "Let me know what you think about..." he paused to tug on Jade's finger to ensure that he had her undivided attention, "the super freak... Rick James."

While the song "Fire and Desire" by Rick James and Tina Marie played, he leaned in towards Jade, turned the music all the way up and whispered to her in her ear so that Decimal couldn't hear. Decimal damn sure did not like that move and his anger instantly spiked as hot as fish grease. Still, he had to respect the game and keep his cool. Otherwise, him and Jade might be walking. Instead of bashing Leo's head in, he leaned back and looked out the window while Leo put the moves on Jade. When they reached Eau Claire, Leo pointed to a very nice house just off the highway under construction.

Next, he lied to Jade and said the house was his but due to noise, he was staying at a motel in town while renovations were being made. Being naïve to the game, she looked at the car he was driving and believed him. Not knowing the truth that everything that he had shown her was cosmetic, and Leo didn't have shit. The car he was driving was a rental. All the crisp $100 bills in his pocket were actually from his monthly military pension check. The motel he mentioned was his actual residence. Still, his darkest secret was that Leo suffered from regular delusions of PTSD. He quickly told her that money didn't mean nothing to him, but she was special, and that if she stopped to have one drink and sent Decimal to the liquor store to grab cash from an ATM and a bottle, that he would give her $500 for just a couple of minutes alone with her to talk. She quickly agreed and texted the proposal to Decimal, who thought nothing about it and looked at Leo as the average old lonely trick. He texted back, "yes!" and asked for directions to the ATM and liquor store from the motel room.

Cold air shot through the motel's deserted parking lot as Leo and Jade exited the car. Before she headed toward the room door, she quickly asked Decimal, "How long will you be?"

He said, "That depends on how long you need to tap his pocket?"

Uncertainty was in her eyes as she asked, "Is twenty minutes too long?"

Decimal replied, "I can work with that. The store is only about a block and a half from here. I'll stall for a minute. Just be ready when I get back and if he comes up with any money games, I am taking this Lincoln and will run it through Juvee's chop shop."

She asked, "What about his bank card?"

Decimal smiled as he sat down in the plush driver seat and said, "Oh, I am sorry, I must have lost it!" and then he pulled off.

Jade just shook her head as she turned towards the room door. Her heart jumped after that she had turned expecting to see Leo waiting for her at the door. Instead, all she saw were the whites of his eyes in the darkness at the back of the room. Consumed by a momentarily blast of fear, she quickly yelled after her husband, "Ra'zee!"

Not seeing her, he hit the corner and sped off to the store. When she looked back at the room, the light was on, and Leo was standing in the doorway smiling. He held up two plastic cups with vodka in them and asked, "Jade, is everything alright? You coming in?"

Although a deafening scream resounded in her soul that she should not go into that room, the whisper of idiocy prevailed as she told herself, "Its only twenty minutes" as she grabbed the cup and walked into the room. The room itself was a pig sty. The more Jade stumbled through cheap plastic liquor bottles and various empty 24 once beer cans, she noticed the molded food shelf bread bags on the dresser top. The realization settled in that she was in a bad place.

Leo dug through one of the dresser drawers until he found what looked like a filthy baby sweat sock. From the bottom of it, he pulled out a wax piece of paper that had about two grams of powder cocaine in it. Jade said nothing as he crushed about one fifth of it and snorted it quickly like a Hoover vac. After a couple of drips water to drain his nose, he shouted, "Wooo!" like Ric Flair and smacked the dresser top hard.

In a heartbeat, his whole demeanor changed as the paranoia settled in. It was as if he was in Saigon and behind enemy lines and that Jade was a spy whore who was about to tell his military company's position. He started pacing back and forth and then blocked the room door and told her to get in the bathroom. Scared to death, she didn't hesitate to obey his command as she asked calmly, "Leo, honey. Are you okay? Maybe you should play some music?"

Leo grabbed her by the hair and yanked her toward the bathroom as he yelled, "Get in there now!"

Some of Jade's drinks splashed in her eye as Leo smacked the cup from her hand. Blinded by the intense burn of the vodka, she struggled to see Leo's hand before it gripped her throat as he said, "I will cut your throat before you can scream one word. Now, tell me, who the hell is Ra'zee? What did you tell him about me and how many of his boys are out there waiting to ambush me?"

Before she could answer, he slapped her so hard that a long drool of saliva came out of her mouth. Immediately, the side of her face went numb as his massive hand covered the entire side of her head. Every nerve in her jaw became powerless and unresponsive as if under Novocain at the dentist. Just as she threw up her arms in fear of the next blow from him, Decimal pulled back into the parking lot. He had forgotten to get the pin number to Leo's bank card. Jade scrambled into the bathroom and tried to block the door. With one kick from Leo, the thin door cracked at the hinge and buckled in.

When Decimal got out of the car, he could hear Jade's loud screams inside the room and the repeated kicks to the bathroom door. Just as the bathroom door fell in on top of her, Decimal kicked in the room door and charged at Leo. Marines are taught to improvise and to quickly adapt in all situations and to overcome. The specialized training they undergo to be combat ready makes them very dangerous adversaries, especially in close quarters. with catlike instincts, Leo spun around, and all his training kicked in. He immediately crouched low and hit Decimal in his pelvic bone and toppled him. As he fell forward, Decimal threw a solid jab to Leo's left eye and rocked him into the dresser. Leo instantly countered with an open hand Marine punch to the throat while Jade crawled from under the door to aid her husband. In a struggle for air behind the blow to his throat, Decimal quickly realized that Leo would be a handful, so he wrapped him up. While they rolled and tussled between the bed and the dresser, Jade stomped Leo in his head, but that only seemed to aggravate him more. Now, he began to growl like a rabid dog and moan like a wolf. Next, he started to viciously bite Decimal's shoulder. When her husband yelled from the molars that pierced his flesh, Jade panicked, grabbed an empty glass one-liter vodka bottle from the garbage can by the bed. She broke the bottleneck off on the edge of the nightstand as a deranged look filled her eyes as fear for her husband's life consumed her.

"Ahhh, get off of him!" she yelled as she stabbed Leo in the base of the neck. Strangulation like convulsions filled Decimal's ear as Jade twisted the two-inch-thick glass bottleneck and snapped the joint between Leo's cerebral cortex and spine. With bulging eyes, his grip weakened to a mild twitch. Slowly, he sat up and reached for the bottle neck at the base of his skull. Decimal quickly shoved Leo off his body. When he fell backwards and hit the floor, his body froze in an arch. The sheer weight of Leo's own torso pushed the glass bottleneck clear through the base of his skull and partly out his mouth.

Chapter 16
Jaded Claws

————————◦○◦——————————

Blood from the bottleneck that she corkscrewed into the base of his skull saturated three of her broken fingernails. Huge teardrops remained frozen in her eyes like the gumdrop tears of a child too afraid to climb out of their bed at night. Paralyzed from the surge of adrenaline, she shook with tiny tremors as the realization of what she had just done in a fit of rage settled in. Decimal sat up half winded between the bed and the dresser to the look of his wife in shambles. There was still somewhat of a deranged look in her eyes as electrical flashes of light green skipped past the windows of her mind. Slowly, the initial shock dissipated as the realization of the fact that she had just killed a man took its place.

"Hey, hey, hey, hey you had no choice. He would have

killed both of us," he said as he crawled over Leo's body to her. Jade just shook with confusion as she mumbled a tangled mess of gibberish while he held her tightly in his arms.

"He said he wanted to have a drink. He was going to kill you. I should clean up my drink. Then I heard you scream, and I lost it!" she cried.

"Yeah, and you did what you had to do to protect your family right? Anybody would have done the same thing in your shoes. I would have made him lick his own blood from the heel of my boot for biting me had you not stabbed him with that broken bottle. Besides, he actually killed himself when he fell backwards onto the bottle, not you."

A sobering thought settled in her mind as she sniffled through short gasps of air and tears as she said, "Wha-a-t? I didn't kill him?"

Decimal took a deep breath and said, "No beautiful, technically you didn't. But none of that will matter if we are both found here in this room with his dead body. At the very least, we would be looking at 3rd degree reckless homicide. That carries a mandatory twelve-to-twenty-year sentence in prison. We have got to get out of here."

Jade asked, "What about him?"

Decimal said, "He is coming too. We can't leave him here. There would be too much criminal negligence. Plus, the BCA report would definitely yield some type of DNA linking his death to me. With my jacket from

Milwaukee and the Twin Cities, all of the batteries, shootings, and times that I have been questioned, the courts here in Wisconsin would fry my ass. Plus, unlike Minnesota, Wisconsin has got a truth in sentencing law over here that requires you to serve 100 percent of your time. I don't even want to begin to think about what that would mean for us."

Since the dawn of time, panic induced actions have given birth to some of the most horrendous crimes against humanity ever regretted by man. Panic moved Adolf Hitler to build places like Auschwitz in beautiful German neighborhoods to hide his hatred for Jews that he had labeled Christ killers. Panic of being discovered as a serial killer mover Jeffrey Dahmer to bake his Milwaukee apartment with powerful industrial cleaning agents to mask the scent of the dead bodies he continued to collect and dismember. This way, he could bask in their terror as he relived each slaying, night after night. Panic: it has spawned numerous shootings by poorly trained police officers. Ones without warrant have killed many unarmed civilians across the nation sparking outrage and a unified cry for a civic purge.

As panic seized both of their minds as to what to do with Leo's body, a dark thought crossed Decimal's mind and he said, "I think I know what to do. We can restage this scene to make it look like someone else killed Leo, and I think I know just who to copycat. Tell me, do you remember the killings that took place about five years ago? The killer was never caught, and the police gave him the tag name of the Widow Maker."

Jade responded, "Are you sure about this? Tell me some more about this person. He sounds very dangerous."

Frustrated, Decimal exclaimed, "Look, we can do, or I can teach. We don't have time for both."

Jade replied, "Fine, fine, if you think it will work then I am with you. What do you need me to do?"

Decimal quickly said, "Take all of his personal possessions: money, jewelry, ID cards. Grab that blanket from the bed to wrap him up in. We will have to burn his body in a secluded field. That will get rid of our DNA that may be on him. Then, all we have to do is use some small stones to leave the Widow Maker's initials around the top of Leo's head."

Jade jumped and said, "How will we know the right spot around here?"

Decimal shook his head and said, "No, we have to do it around the Twin Cities since it was said to be the backyard of the Widow Maker."

Jade said, "Maybe we should rethink this?"

Decimal's eyes squinted at her as he said, "I know you don't believe those stories, do you? Tag names are just something the police make up when they don't have any leads to actually catch someone. Think about it, if any of those murders were true then why would they just up and stop? As far as I can remember, if a person gets away with committing a crime that they enjoyed doing, then they will do it again. I never met a gunslinger who just up and stopped shooting people or a pimp who just cut off all of his whores. So, what's the likelihood that a serial killer just stopped killing. Slim to none. You know why, because it never happened? At the very least, they'd pick another state, but just up and stop? That's bullshit! Now, come on. Let's get to work. We still have to wipe down this room and clean up the blood on this floor."

Although she felt uncertain, Jade knew that this was not Decimal's first rodeo when it came to ducking the law. So, she followed along with his scheme to outsmart the authorities. After the carpet had been scrubbed, the room wiped down, and somewhat organized to appear looking as if there had been a party in there instead of a tussle, they stood the bathroom door up and stacked all of the empty beer cans and bottles on one side of the dresser top. Lastly, Decimal poured out the last of the cocaine on the nightstand by the bed and made a bunch of thin lines to snort. While they hurried to wrap Leo's body in the blanket from the bed to move him into the trunk of the rental car for transport, one of Leo's massive hands slowly opened then quickly reclosed on a lock of Jade's long hair. Although the hand movement was purely involuntary; a faint impulse triggered by one of the last electrical messages recycling itself through failing synapses in the brain. An uncontrollable shiver resonated across her torso.

Fear filled her almond shaped eyes and her voice quaked as it crackled under her hyperventilating, "He is still alive! Get him off me!" she yelled as she pulled away.

Decimal grabbed her by the arm to get control of her so that he could free her tangled patch of hair that was now trapped in Leo's death grip.

"Hey, hey, calm down. He's dead. His brain is simply misfiring behind the last signals it perceived. Sometimes the head, arms, and legs twitch. Bodies sit straight up as if being called after being dead even in the morgue for several hours. His hand just got tangled up in your hair. You are okay."

Softly, Jade began to cry as he slowly pulled a handful of her hair from between Leo's blood ashy fingers. Decimal could easily tell that she had reached her breaking point. In many ways though, he was impressed at the fact that through all of this chaos, she had shown this much strength. Whatever reservoir of fuel she had left to muster form her tank of perseverance had all dissipated once Leo's eyes popped open and his gaze fell directly into the eyes of Jade. His vacant eyes bulged with fear of impending death and gleamed with clear recognition as to who the fatal blow had actually come from. Patches of fuzzy fog blanketed Jade's mine and flickered morbid images of dark light in the room. Then the multifaceted colors of a spectrum that belonged to an unknown misty aura pulled the two- and one-half pound soul from Leo's body shrouded the bed. It was more than her mind could bear and without further delay, Jade collapsed at the foot of the bed.

Nearly an hour later when she awakened, they were in the car and pulling behind Rosemont Highschool off south Robert Trail in Rosemont, Minnesota. A dense thicket of trees separated the suburban school's property from the townhomes in the back. It was indeed the perfect location in the backyard of the Twin Cities to dispose of Leo's dead body at and remain undetected. The old school property had an outdated video surveillance system. It consisted primarily of three poorly positioned cameras purchased in a set at Radio Shack I 1975. In an effort to reduce teen pregnancy, one was positioned to simultaneously monitor traffic into both the boys and girl's locker room. Another bulky video camera sat above the main doors that overlooked the cafeteria to catch perpetrators that participated in food fights and to discourage bullying as well as physical altercations. The last video camera watched for vandalism in the small side staff parking lot. The Lincoln MKX rocked side to side along the narrow four-wheeler dirt bike path as it squeezed its way deeper and deeper into the dense patch of tall, slender, birch trees. These trees acted like a cocoon to protect the pupal non feeding stage within metamorphosis where one thing dies and something else is born from its destruction. Each tree was speckled with bright white spots and covered with bark peeling in thin papery leaves. Bright beams of light wrapped in dense fog cascaded through the tall slender trees, giving the appearance as though each ray was burning its way through an encasement of dark secrets.

When Mei Wei woke up, the thick cover of the trees had begun to pull darkness over the car. Ra'zee didn't know that she had stared at him for several moments then looked through the flickers of sunlight and made out the passing image of the high school just beyond the trees. While she stretched and adjusted her seat, she asked quietly in a groggy voice, "Where are we?"

Glad that she was awake, he said, "Hey beautiful! I thought you would sleep clean through the night. Anyways, we are up in Rosemont behind the old high school. I thought long and hard about a good spot to leave Leo's body at and this one came to mind. I remembered that before we met, I used to meet this one rich kid named Josh here. He was known for throwing these sick banging parties and dating bad ass college chicks. Although he had money, he wanted to sell a little weed at school to boost his tough guy party image. So, I doubled the price on every ounce I sold him just because. There's this pit they dug and put bricks in to burn like a bonfire so they could party out here at night. Since this is Minnesota, that's where I am going to give Leo his Viking funeral at."

Like a flash flood, everything that had happened since they left Milwaukee up until when she passed out came back to her memory and Mei Wei had to throw up. "Stop the car! Stop the car!"

In his mind, Ra'zee wondered if she would ever fully recover mentally from the trauma that he had allowed to come into their life. He knew that he should have never agreed to let some strange man spend time alone with his wife for any price of money. Then, the obvious settled in on him. If he had not doubled back to the room for Leo's pin number for his bank card, then more than likely Mei Wei would be dead now. Even more unnerving was the glare in her eyes when she looked at him briefly then past him and out the window when she woke up. A look that revealed the staggering truth that he had treated her like the average girl in traffic and cast her like fresh bait to trap a wolf. He didn't protect her as his wife, and all of this was his fault. The more she vomited, the more the liquor wore off. Suddenly, he reminded her so much of Xiao Lee. That's when her trust for him quietly died and a subtle contempt grew in her against all men.

CHAPTER 17
OUT OF THE ASHES

When Ra'zee opened the trunk of the car, a horrible stench like a room full of pig intestine at a slaughterhouse, made him step back immediately. With his nose buried deep inside the collar of his jacket, he said, "Damn, I should have remembered to wrap you in plastic first. I forgot all about your bowels letting loose." A rancid puddle of feces had soaked clear through the blanket and the thin black carpet that lined the floor of the trunk. Ra'zee proceeded to pull Leo's body out onto the ground while Mei Wei took several deep breaths in front of the headlights. When she noticed his struggle to remove the body alone, she made her way towards the back of the car to offer help.

When Ra'zee looked up and saw her, he quickly said,

"Maybe you should just wait in the car?"

Jade snapped back, "No, I am good. I just want to hurry up and get this over with so we can get the hell out of here."

Ra'zee said, "Okay, help me sit him up then and pull his legs out of the trunk. Trust me, it will be easier for us to flip him out of the trunk onto the ground. Then, we can drag him over to the pit. Please, try to not touch anything wet."

When Leo's body hit the ground like a fifty-pound bag of potatoes, a small piece of the blanket tore off on the locking mechanism to the trunk. Once they had dragged the body to the edge of the pit, Ra'zee said, "I can take it from here," and headed back to the car. Mei Wei said nothing. She just stood there and stared into the bottom of the pit. Once he got back to the trunk to look for the roadside emergency repair kit, he additionally found a tire air gauge plus a windshield wiper and radiator fluids in the spare tire compartment. He poured out all the windshield wiper fluid. Next, he knocked the metal bulb head from the readers end of the air gauge and emptied the contents into his jacket pocket. Then, he used the rugged end of the metal piece left in his hand to scrape a hole in the side of the plastic container. After several minutes of cutting through the side of the jug while constantly turning it, he removed the bottom half. Next, he slid under the driver's side of the car and used the tip of his shirt to twist the small half inch screw plug from the oil pan. After he had filled the plastic container, he slid out from under the car, gathered a couple of branches, and headed back to the pit.

Mei Wei asked curiously, "What are you going to do with those?"

Slightly winded, Ra'zee whispered back, "Oil is flammable. I needed something to get the fire going."

Mei Wei just looked at him. She had never known this side of him and now she wished that she didn't. She could tell that he had killed before. Now, she wondered if he would kill again. He threw several small branches into the pit. Then, he poured a little oil on top, added a few more branches, then rolled Leo on top of the stack. He couldn't help to notice the catatonic look on Mei Wei's face when Leo slid down into the 3 ft deep concave pit. Pulling the flare stick out of his pocket, he turned toward her and softly said, "Are you sure you don't want to wait in the car? I think you've been traumatized enough for one day."

Mei Wei didn't even look his way. Coldly, she responded, "No, I want to see this so just get on with it Decimal."

Without hesitation, he said, "Okay then Jade, let's get this over with."

Decimal tossed two more large branches on top of Leo. Next, he collected twenty-seven medium sized rocks from the ground and used them to put the initials TWM, for the Widow Maker, at the top of the pit by Leo's head.

While each rock was being set in the earth for burial markings, tiny vibrations of sound behind each thud of the stones hitting the dirt were carried miles away deep in the bayous. In the dark, secluded, decadent attic, the force of every stone that was set resonated across Carlos' flesh. Cold beads of sweat formed across his face, arms, and chest. Profusely, he started to sweat.

When Decimal leaned over the pit and proceeded to uncover Leo's face, Jade asked, "What the hell are you doing?"

With the broken tire air gauge raised about Leo's head, Decimal quickly turned towards Jade and said, "Oh, I forgot to tell you. The Widow Maker always takes the eyes of his victims."

Jade whispered, "Are you seriously going to do that?"

Decimal whispered back through his teeth while he turned his head back to remeasure his target, "I don't want to, but it is either him or us."

In four swift blows, he stabbed the tire gauge twice through each eye, wiped it off on the blanket, and laid it on Leo's chest. Jade had seen enough and took off running back to the car. Decimal stood up, wrapped the handkerchief in his pocket around the end of the last branch by his foot like a torch and dipped it in the remaining oil. He cracked the flare, laid it right on Leo's chest with the torch, and poured the last bit of oil across him. As he ran back to the car, he noticed Jade in a ball-like position in her seat looking the opposite way out of the window. The fiery red glow grew in the reflection of her window. The crackle of wood that released a sea of embers filtered high into the sky. A swirl of ashes carried by a gust of wind blew swiftly through the trees as Decimal sped in reverse back across the dirt path. By the time he pulled back out onto south Robert Trail, the fire was in full blaze.

Immediately, Decimal called Juvenile and told him he had a pickup, and that he needed him to send a flatbed tow truck by his house with a car cover. While their phone call dragged on all Mei Wei could think about was a shower, a cup of hot tea, and a change of clothes. For even though the outfit she was wearing was brand new, she had every intention of going home and burning it. Whatever she could do to bury the last twenty-four hours of her life, she was prepared to do. Then suddenly, it dawned on her. All of this started from trying to calm their nerves behind a surprise note from her mother. A call that she had still not made. A call that she definitely wasn't prepared to return now. For no matter how much time had elapsed between them, Youa Wei Lee was still her mother.

Motherly instincts had already told her that something was terribly wrong with her only child Mei Wei. As a child, Mei Wei had never been good at lying to her mother. Her external cues were that she laughed for no apparent reason, fidgeted around, avoided making eye contact, and nervously tapped her right foot on the floor. If by some act of God she could divert all of those cues, how exactly would she explain the closed right eye that resulted from when Leo smacked the hell out of her? Then, there was a discolored bruise on her left cheek that had already begun to show signs of purple and orange spots. Even more, her mom would instantly blame Ra'zee and ask her father Ip Vang to have someone kill him for it. Slowly, Mei Wei placed both of her hands on her face. She felt like her life was in complete chaos and her face was one of the many evidences of that.

989 miles, away in the condemned attic space, the eyes of Carlos, who sat cross-legged on the floor, slowly opened and burned red hot with spite and contempt. Several faint beams of light pierced alongside of the heavy oak pillars that created the attic's sturdy old structure. He couldn't explain it, but somehow, he knew that an unwanted force like a car crash, had verged with his eternal destiny. Suddenly, the mortar of the brick wall cracked behind him and Carlos could hear the voice of his Egyptian Blackness echo deep within a cavernous hallway. The familiar bone chilling presence of Animus shrouded him in a decadent darkness as his nostrils filled with the god-awful stench of blood mixed with dead rodents. The sound of Carlos' panting breaths grew steadily in the room as dust filled wind blew in behind him.

While Maria approached the attic door with Jaysiah on her hip, the Widow Maker stood over him and asked, "What plagues your mind my young padawan? You seem deeply distraught as if under great emotional conflict."

Carlos hesitated, then said, "I cannot explain it, but for some reason I keep thinking about the old toolshed back in our vineyard."

Upon hearing that, the Widow Maker was reminded of the conversation between him and McIntyre the day of their flight into the bayous. With the hour of his return drawing nigh, he whispered to Carlos, "Mother awaits us. Therefore, choose a dwelling in a port city for her sake. Watch from there until the spider has weaved its web."

He turned to cross back over just as Maria opened the attic door and began to climb the steps. The wall scraped the floor as it slid through mortar chips and dirt to reclose. Carlos turned around and walked towards the top of the stairs. The Latin inscription, "Lux Ab Exitium Velle Venere" echoed in the attic just as he met Maria at the top of the steps.

Maria asked, "What did you just say?"

Carlos ignored her questions and said, "For five years, we have been hiding down here in the bayous. I cannot explain it, but I feel that it is necessary that I return to the Twin Cities. A lot has changed, our family has grown, and I don't know what to expect when I get there. All I know is that I must go. I will understand if you want to stay here until I return."

Maria said, "You are my family. Where you go, I go. Plus, I want to be there in case you need me."

Carlos gently placed his hand on Maria's arm as he

looked into his son's eyes and said, "You want to go and meet your grandma? She is going to be very happy to see you. Maybe not so much me? Especially not after how things were when your mom and I left."

Maria was about to tell Carlos that she had recently spoken to McIntyre and that she didn't take it so well. Instead, she said, "Let's get out of this attic before something bites this boy and we have to go to the hospital. Plus, if we are leaving, then I better start packing. When are we leaving?

Carlos looked at her piercingly through the darkness and said, "At first light."

Maria was shocked that he wanted to leave so soon. Nevertheless, she didn't complain, but simply said, "Well, sounds like we are traveling light," then she turned and headed back down the stairs. When she didn't hear his footsteps behind her, she stopped to turn around and asked, "Are you coming?"

Carlos said, "I just need to do one thing first. It will take me less than a minute, then I will be downstairs."

Maria looked at Carlos briefly and wondered just what he could possibly be doing in the condemned attic. Remembering her promise to not question him, she turned and said, "Well, I am going to pack a couple changes of clothes for me and the kids. I reckon you probably already have a bag packed. Just out of curiosity, how have you thought about what we are going to tell Uncle Cedric about how long we will be gone?"

As Carlos disappeared from the top of the stairs,

his voice trailed off behind him. He moved across the rotten floor to an old bookshelf in the corner that held thirteen small white boxes from his mother's house, evenly spread out across four shelves flush to the edge. Over the creek of each step, he said, "For now, we will just tell him that we are going on a little road trip to see some of my relatives and should be back in about two weeks."

Maria responded distractedly over Jaysiah trying to touch the molded walls, "Okay, sounds good to me. Jaysiah keep your hands to yourself. Eww, it stinks in here."

As the door clicked closed, Carlos reached the bookshelf. Quietly, he stood there for a moment and held the palm of his hand open about six inches from the boxes. Slowly, he closed his eyes and began to move his hand across each row as if he could somehow sense the content of each box. Snapshots of gruesome killings and soul wrenching cries filled his mind as his hand glided past each box. Halfway across the third shelf, his hand stopped at the second box. He opened it and removed an hourglass filled with crushed vertebrae that was ground into a granulated powder. After sitting it upright on the shelf to start the clock of his return, he left.

CHAPTER 18
DEPRAVITY

———⟡———

C hoice Theory states that there are many axioms but only two that you should strongly consider: 1. The only person's behavior that you can truly control at any given time is your own; 2. The only thing in this life that you can actually offer to anyone else is information. This becomes a self –contradictory statement, nothing more than a paradox. A mere assertion based on a valid deduction from normal premises. The rules quickly change under extraordinary circumstances, especially when it comes to a loved one or a spouse. The new expectation are that those closest to us will intervene on our behalf and make better choices for us that under current pretenses we cannot make for ourselves.

In all of their chaotic behavior, this is what Mei

Wei desired most of all from Ra'zee. Instead, all she continually got was more coaching from her personal tour guide into depravity Decimal. She was amazed at the fact that in the midst of all of this, it seemed to be business as usual for him. Even though they had travelled way off the reservation of normality, he seemed to be quite comfortable in his surroundings. It was not normal behavior when she corkscrewed the neck of a liquor bottle into Leo's skull, then aided her husband to wrap up his corpse and transport it out of state. To stage a homicide scene and evade the state of Wisconsin's truth in sentencing laws.

By the time they got home and got Juvenile to dispose of the car, Mei Wei's soul had begun to quietly recoil inside of her. After her shower, she quiescently sat in a chair at the dining room table, sipped her tea, and stared aimlessly out the window. Dressed in all white, like a patient recovering at a psych ward, she pulled her feet up into the chair, wrapped her arms around her legs, and attempted to rest her head on her knees. With her face tender from the swelling, she shifted her head position several times before resorting to her chin. Tiny vapors of steam arose from her teacup as she gently tugged the little string to dip the bag. The typical humdrum of the neighborhood seemed to be untouched, which was comforting in some regards. For it whispered that just maybe, they could move on and put this truly terrible experience behind them. As she leaned forward in order to check to make sure that Leo's rental car was actually gone from the parking spot in front of their house, the teacup slipped from her hand and shattered on the floor. She noticed that a police squad car was parked in its place and two uniformed officers were approaching their door.

When the cup hit the floor, Ra'zee quickly looked over at her from the sofa and asked, "Are you okay?"

Mei Wei's eye bulged with fear as she struggled to speak while pointing outside.

Ra'zee asked again, "What's wrong?" as he quickly muted the volume on the TV and came to see what her had so shook with fear.

Finally, she spoke, "The police are outside!"

Ra'zee extended his hands toward her in a calming gesture as he said, "Calm down." Then, over the heavy knock on the front door, he continued, "I called them while you were in the shower to report our car stolen from in front of the house. That way, we are eliminated from having been in Madison, Wisconsin all together."

Mei Wei sighed long and hard out of pure weariness. "Dammit, why didn't you tell me that you had called them, and couldn't that have waited?" She stormed off to the bedroom and slammed the door behind her.

Ra'zee yelled behind her on his way to the front door, "I am sorry beautiful, I forgot."

Mei Wei sat in the room and listened to the conversation between Ra'zee and the police officers who he had invited inside. While one officer questions Ra'zee about possibly when the vehicle had been stolen, the other one looked around. Ra'zee did his best impersonation of the typical angry but respectable suburban homeowner who had just had his personal property stolen from his home, and who expected them to find the culprit immediately since he was a taxpayer. The other officer wasn't buying it so easily. He had heard the door slam prior to their delayed entry and was now looking at the broken teacup on the floor by the dining room table that still had faint vapors of steam coming up from it. Noticing the small, wet footprints on the lightly dusted floor that came from the shower and Ra'zee wearing roughly a size 11 men's shoes, Officer Mosley, who was training to become a detective, thought the setting looked awfully like the house had been vacant for a few days, but he said nothing.

To verify his suspicions, he said, "Maybe your wife saw something out of place? Maybe an individual or a car in the neighborhood that seemed a little out of place? Is she around?"

Ra'zee, not thinking that the cop was looking beyond his complaint, responded, "She has the flu and has been in bed all day."

The cop responded, "Does she now? Mind if I go outside to have a look around? Maybe something else is missing?" With several newspapers on the porch and a mailbox full of mail, he knew that they had not been there for several days. The question was where had they exactly been and why conceal that?

Over the next couple of months, Mei Wei's attitude

became dark, cynical and unnerving. A cocoon that she would hide in so that she didn't have to discuss how lost she felt inside. The bitter truth about hiding in the darkness of one's own heart is that you eventually become hidden even more from yourself. What was initially to be her ally became her worst distraction and consumed her in the form of an eye for an eye muse. For in the darkness, she lost a desire to work and was subsequently fired. She sought solace in tequila and burrowed herself in retail therapy.

After a very fast paced lifestyle with no income, in a relatively short amount of time, the bills piled up and desperation settled in. There had been no whisper of any further investigation behind Leo's death. The farced witticisms of Decimal and Jade had proven quite successful to fool the authorities once. So, it was only natural that over the course of time that they slide into the normal line of criminal thinking that most criminals with their instant success rate do. A line of thinking that says, "We got away with it once. Surely, we can get away with it again." This distorted perception quickly evolved into a deadly tactic with Jade being the bait to allure men into their devious tap, plunder their possessions, and pass off the blame onto the Widow Maker.

Day by day, Ra'zee grew to be more vicious than his mentor Double Cross. His actions showed that by any means necessary, he was going to get paid, even at the cost of Mei Wei, his wife. He had justified in his mind that if she wasn't giving him any of her cookies anymore, that there had to be come crumbs on someone else's pillow. Therefore, if she was out tricking off, why do it for play when you can do it for profit? Rapidly, Mei Wei's morals became as tainted as the bottom of her dirty feet. A debased mind devolved within her to where she liked how she looked and loved her lifestyle. She even admired how Decimal competed aggressively and heartlessly in his murderous game of monopoly. From sunup to sundown, he did all he could do to lock and slide the dice, and to repeatedly stack a certain number of the odds in their favor. He laughed when he had the opportunity to take someone's money. He traded and cut deals to buy information on suspecting targets that he called a lick. Then, he quickly converted the information into an unsuspecting encounter with his temptress Jade. At the end of each night when he had taken all of the money, drugs, and jewelry he could find, along with swiftly ending the occasional life to amass their fortune, he sat in disgust and thought about all the possibilities of the trifling things that Jade had done all day while she scrubbed herself down in the shower.

With all his keen ability to read streets, somehow, he missed the bold print of his own future obituary that read he was on his way to ending up just like his predecessor Double Cross. Whom, in the end, just like all who have ever played this deadly game, he sadly removed his blood monopoly crown, arose from the table and placed all his winnings from the deceptive allure of the street life back into the box. There, the titles and prizes would await and taunt those that passed by like the pounding sound of the bass drum, like from Jumanji, until a curious fool dare open the box, roll the dice, and start the game again. For the players may change, but the game remains the same.

It was over the course of this same time frame that Mei Wei and Youa Wei had settled into a regular routine of meeting twice a week at a café for tea. It was apparent by her mother's facial expression that Youa Wei felt increasingly embarrassed by Mei Wei's public appearance. She wore very short, skintight, spaghetti strapped t-shirt dresses. She wreaked of alcohol and made numerous trips in and out of the café's bathroom barefoot revealing the bottom of her dirty feet as she walked. Youa Wei would constantly mumble corrective behavioral phrases to her by which Mei Wei was embarrassed. So, she decided to sever all recently renewed ties with her.

Youa Wei sternly said to her one afternoon, "Daughter, I had hoped that you would eventually come to your senses, stop parading yourself around half naked every day, and put off this shameful lifestyle. It is embarrassing amongst the other families to have a daughter that has been arrested as much as you. Sometimes, I wonder if I've been wasting my time."

A tear fell from Mei Wei's eye as she told her mother," I am sick and tired of every time that we meet for tea that you look at me like I just pulled a used condom from between my legs, in the back of a New York City taxicab. I am so sick of your under-the-breath-comments. I thought you would have accepted the fact that I had changed. I am no longer the sweet little girl that sat back and watched as you moved that man into our house, and then allowed him to hit me and toss me outside in the rain like I was nothing."

In desperation, Youa Wei tried to plead, "Daughter, wait. I was wrong. I wasn't there for you, but I am trying to be here for you now."

Mei Wei snapped, "Save it!" as she sneered at her. Then she smiled mockingly at her while she pointed her finger in her mom's face and said, "I remember you taught me to never live in the problem, but rather live for the solution. Well, here's mine, and I am done with you! You ended it last time, and I was a fool to let you back into my life."

They stood up while Mei Wei collected her things. Then, desperation consumed Youa Wei, and she told Mei Wei about her dream. Instantly, Xiao Lee's words were proven true. She dismissed everything her mom said as eastern mysticism and nonsense. Quietly, she removed the family pendant from her neck, set it on the table and walked off barefoot while trying to pull down her snug fitted body dress. Decimal had just pulled up at the end of the parking lot. With their car having been stolen in Madison, Wisconsin, he was left with no choice but to pull out his old school Electra 225 for transport. He had rarely driven it since he stopped hustling in order to settle with and please Mei Wei. But now, all of that had changed. Every morning, he was like a snot nose kid on his new green machine big wheel.

When he noticed Mei Wei crying, he got out of the car and ran to meet her. While she laid her head on his chest and cried, Decimal put on his UV tinted Cartier sunglasses and smiled at her mom. He knew that he didn't have to worry about her sabotaging all his hard work anymore. Just as they made it to the car and Ra'zee opened the car door for her, two detective cars swerved into the parking lot and boxed them in. Officers quickly exited their squad cars with pistols drawn and yelled, "Ra'zee and Mei Wei Lajoune, aka Decimal and Jade. You are both under arrest for the kidnapping, murder, and mutilation of Leonard Johns, plus several other crimes."

CHAPTER 19
FEAST OF SOULS

E l Dia de los Muertos: The Day of the Dead (Mexico). Ching Ming: Sweeping Tomb Day (China). Walpurgisnacht (Germany). All Saints Day Fiesta (Philippines). Mischief Night (United States) or as we call it, Halloween.

For years, many have been under the belief that lawlessness is permissible on the one night a year when the veil between the natural and the spirit realms is torn. Such a night is legendary for recompensing old transgressions fourfold. Also, but not for the weak in the stomach, was the tenure to slight in a purge for the night.

It was a little after 6 pm when an unusual dense fog began to build and settled low on the ground across downtown Rochester, Minnesota. The air outside was crisp and gave the perfect ambience for Zombie Fest. This was a time when the inhabitants of this small city would crawl, stumble, drag themselves, moan and walk contorted as if they had all become part of Michael Jackson's Thriller video set.

Light tremors shook the tiny house on Center Street as a freight train passed by. Upstairs in the attic, Carlos sat cross legged on the floor in front of a barren brick wall. The low echo of him chanting the Latin inscription, "Lux Ab Exitium Velle Venere," to invoke the terrifying presence of his Egyptian Blackness, the Widow Maker, whispered over the playful chatter of the children downstairs. What he initially perceived to have been only a few minutes was in actual a time lapse of about two hours into the night. A chill had set in the attic and Carlos' eyes grew heavy. As he began to nod off, the familiar chime of six nickels falling to the ground filled his hearing and his vision grew hazy. The wall cracked before him, and a hellish stench filled the room. The doorway to a cavernous hall appeared before him from the other side.

The Widow Maker crossed over and told Carlos, "This is the one night per year that I can walk openly in public. Therefore, tonight you shall witness from behind the veil until sunrise. Make haste and dress according to what I bid you. Do not forget to prepare the old tools of our original syringe filled with battery acid and our first scalpel. For this town shall bathe in true light as I recompense all of the sins of their fathers upon their sons."

"Yes, yes!" responded Carlos in a clear and conspiring voice. "I will make all of your necessary preparations at once."

While Maria rotated all the kids in and out of their nightly bath time routines, Carlos slowly eased out of the back door into the alley between third and second street, behind center street. He crossed over the railroad tracks just past Well Haven Music Company store from 15th and Broadway North. There, he noticed a billboard for Hanny's men and women's wear, located at 19 1st Avenue SW. Not really knowing the city and being unsure where else he might acquire dress attire for the Widow Maker, he went there. When nothing suited him in there, he spotted a mom-and-pop bridal store through the window just a couple doors down. Inside the small bridal boutique, he found the perfect Steele gray and white colored suit. The pearl white dress shirt and pants bore light grey stitches. They matched exquisitely with the thick square of the golden belt buckle and hard sole white dress shoes with grey laces. Carlos selected a pair of gold cufflinks that reflected beautifully at three quarters of an inch from below the sleeves of his suit coat. As his fingers coursed across the fine knit fabric of the suit, the Widow Maker whispered low under his breath, "The marriage feast of the damned."

A petite, very attractive, older woman in her sixties that tended the store approached and said to him, "You have chosen very well, and those cufflinks accent this suit perfectly. There is, however, a couple more accessories that will be sure to catch every eye in the room."

While looking in the dress mirror, the Widow Maker responded, "Do tell us what you have in mind."

The woman handed him a cotton pair of light gray gloves and a pearl white fedora style brim with a red silk bank around it. Lastly, she gave him a red silk handkerchief, tucked it in his vest pocket, and said, "You look marvelous. Are you perhaps the groom?"

The Widow Maker responded rather coy, "No, but I am the guest of honor."

Later on that night, during Zombie Fest it was like plucking choice fruit from a coveted tree, as the Widow Maker slaughtered several victims in public. Due to the day's events, some had witnessed signs of struggles or victims laid out by stores, shops, and parade rest areas. They thought nothing more of it other than another staged scene as they applauded and commented to each other that it was some of the best work that they had ever seen. The Widow Maker relished in their ignorance and actually engaged a group of teens after one drunken girl commented on how real the blood splatter looked across his sleeves, suit coat, and shoes, and that the dripping effect from the scalpel was a cool signature mark.

A high school freshman in the crowd trying to impress the drunken senior commented to her, "My brother in college makes the best fake blood ever. All he uses is red food dye, water, and a little bit of cornstarch." then, he foolishly looked rather smug at the Widow Maker and said, "Yeah, and it looks exactly like that fake blood."

The Widow Maker responded chillingly at him while his gaze deepened into his eyes, "I assure you I use no props. Plus, why ruin the real McCoy for mere theatre?"

The young man looked at him awkwardly as fear crawled across his flesh. He said nothing else as they walked off. However, the gaze of the Widow Maker rested firmly on him. Halfway down the street, when he looked back and noticed the bone chilling stare of the Widow Maker still on him, Carlos waved tauntingly at him with his pinky finger and proceeded towards him through the crowd. Panic enveloped him as a deafening scream shattered his senses. His natural fight or flight response for survival kicked in and like a drunken idiot, he charged through the crowd toward the Widow Maker. Surprised at how he took off running like a mad man, his classmates yelled after him, "Josh, where are you going?"

They then followed him through the crowd while asking each other, "What the hell got into him?"

The drunk girl named Makayla, whom he had a crush on, joked and said, "He probably remembered his curfew and ran home?"

The Widow Maker, on the other hand, smiled invigoratingly at him as he said to himself, "Not very smart, are we? This one is full of raw potential like a lump of clay is to the potter's wheel. He may be a worthy student in a few years. Unless he incites my wrath, and I am left with no choice except to fillet him like a catfish right here and now."

Distracted momentarily by knocking down flat a stubborn toddler running from his mother, Josh took his eyes off of the Widow Maker for a quick second. When he looked back up, Carlos was gone. When his friends finally caught up, they asked, "What's going on dude? Why did you take off like that? You are really freaking us out."

Josh said, "That crazy looking guy from earlier, in the white suit, was eyeballing me like he was going to Hannibal Lector me."

Makayla scolded at him and said, "And for some reason, you thought it was a good idea to charge right at him because?"

Josh just shrugged his shoulders in embarrassment and said, "I wasn't thinking clearly. I felt like I had to do something. So, I got amped up, about to go WWE all over his ass."

Makayla said, "I must admit you are a dumb ass, but still pretty brave for a freshman."

His boys began shouting, "Josh, Josh, Josh," like they were at a football rally.

Makayla walked over, grabbed his hand and pushed him to lead the crowd down the street. "Come on Roman Reigns. I am getting cold, and you are buying me a hot chocolate."

Feeling like the man, Josh smiled, looked up and

whispered, "Oh God, thank you!"

While the other students were starting to tease him, another girl in their group looked over in the direction that Josh had ran earlier and said, "Hey guys, if Josh is right, then where did he go?"

As they looked throughout the crowd for a sign of the white and grey suit that the Widow Maker wore, Makayla noticed a little girl, no more than six years old. She was standing by herself, on the sidewalk, next to an empty baby carriage. As she moved toward the child to see if the little girl was okay, she noticed blood covering the little girl's Sketcher sneakers with a trail of small, bloodied footprints leading from them back into the alley.

Makayla asked, "Hey, are you okay? Where's your mommy?"

The little girl said nothing but pointed behind her into the alley.

Josh said, "Makayla, stay here with her. I am going to check this out."

Makayla shouted back at him while he slowly walked off into the narrow alley," Josh wait, we should find help!"

Josh kept going until he saw the feet of a woman wearing a light brown shredded dirty rag dress behind a garbage can. Then, he heard the cries of an infant coming from the side of the garbage can close to the ground. There, sitting on the ground, in a puddle of urine, with her baby in her lap, was a young woman.

Her big toes and thumbs had been cut off. Three highly polished nickels replaced each of her missing eyes. A fully loaded heroin needle was still in her arm. The baby was untouched and stopped crying as soon as Josh picked her up. When he emerged from the alley holding the child, Makayla asked, "Where did she come from?"

Josh said, "Mom, in the alley. Trust me, you do not want to go in there." Makayla took the baby from Josh and placed her in the carriage.

"Come on, we need to go find help." When they turned to meet their friends, they wanted details about where the kids came from and where their mother was. Horrifying screams began to ring out from several different locations along the festival's route. One by one, a trail of massacred bodies were discovered that night.

When Carlos returned undetected back to the house, he found Maria and kids already in bed. He placed the Widow Maker's suit back into its protective bag and hung it up in the attic. Then, he quickly showered and joined Maria in bed. When he laid down, he did not know that her eyes were wide open. She had only just laid down when she heard him come through the backdoor downstairs. Her thoughts scattered across her mind like the legs of a centipede, intricate in its own movement, crawling in different directions. As she resisted the courage to ask him where he had been all night, the faint sound of multiple sirens crackled in the air. She could feel it in her stomach that something horrible had happened. Flashbacks of all that she had heard and saw over the last five years flooded her mind instantly. She folded a pillow over her head to try to drown out the sound of the sirens that whispered outside in the night. Forcefully, she squeezed the pillow around her head so tight until all she heard was the pulsating heartbeat in her mind against the thud in her chest. Eventually, she lost consciousness in her own thoughts.

When she awoke in the morning, she felt mentally disoriented lying-in bed alone. The house was totally quiet. The strange surroundings made her wonder where she was at. A thick emptiness hung in the air that made her cringe as she quietly screamed inside. Fuzzy minded and not sure what was happening, she jumped up and ran downstairs, but no one was there. While pouring a glass of milk, she noticed a partial set of bloodied footprints on the floor that came past the refrigerator. She left the carton of milk on the table and slowly followed the set of footprints all the way up the stairs to the attic door. Inside, the footprints led straight to the shoes that were beneath the Widow Maker's suit inside the clear protective liner in the corner. Slowly, she backed out of attic and went to clean up the house.

CHAPTER 20
DARK LABYRINTHS

B y the time Decimal and Jade arrived at the Brooklyn Park Police Department, a barrage of news trucks from several news station along with a growing crowd of spectators had already lined the sidewalk to the parking lot. An armed detail of uniformed officers along with Captain Vasquez standing firmly in the middle, established a secure perimeter to provide the two detective cars in-route access to the precinct. When the nose of the two squad cars reached the barricade of blue uniforms, the flicker of cameras taking pictures and applause from the crowd erupted. Several reporters shouted questions related to the Widow Maker slaying at the cars. Their cameramen tried to take clear pictures of the two suspects in separate squad cars behind the dark tint of the windows. When they exited the squad cars, Jade tried to hide her face.

Decimal yelled while she peeked at him as if she would never see him again, "They ain't got nothing on us! Don't tell them nothing! You hear me? Do not even talk to them!"

A hotshot rookie Detective named Matthews who recently transferred up from the most violent district in Memphis, Tennessee called Pussy Valley, quickly shuttled them inside and placed them into separate interrogation rooms. In the hallway outside of the interrogation room, Captain Vasquez asked Detective Matthews, "Are you sure about this?"

With an overly confident smile, he said, "Cap, trust me, these two are the Widow Maker that you've been looking for. That's why you've never been able to get a clear physical match as to if the Widow Maker was a man or a woman. Trust me Cap, everything fits these two. Especially the forensic evidence of Mei Wei Lajoune's lipstick on the cup found by the bed at Leonard John's motel room in Eau Claire, Wisconsin. Then, the tire thread of the MKX rental car registered to Johns that was found stripped and abandoned on the east side of St. Paul. They were an exact match to the car tracks found on a four-wheeler bike path not too far from where John's body was discovered mutilated and burned behind Rosemont Highschool."

Officer Mosley cut in, "Captain Vasquez, the preliminary findings from forensics going over the stripped car frame revealed that a piece of cloth was found in the locking mechanism to the trunk. It appears to match the style of bedspreads used at the motel in Eau Claire, Wisconsin. Which mean it may have torn off from the bedspread Johns was wrapped up in. Now, judging by the 127-pound frame of Mrs. Lajoune, I don't believe she could have lifted that body alone. Which, although circumstantial, places Decimal as her accomplice.

Captain Vasquez replied, "Great work, keep me posted. I have got to prepare a press release."

As he turned to head toward his office, Matthews asked, "Hey Cap, what about that vacant Lead Detective position?"

Captain Vasquez stopped, looked back, and responded, "Get me a confession and it is yours." As he continued to his office, he couldn't quite put his finger on it, but something gnawed at his conscious. Call it good old fashion training or a cop's gut instincts behind thirty plus years on the force, but there was something about this murder and the string of robberies that didn't line up. They all had the characteristics of the Widow Maker but seemed to be lacking depth of his dark psyche. He knew that Matthews was a good detective. He also knew how badly he wanted the Lead Detective position. There was entirely too much at stake and he could not let this get screwed up on his watch. He went in his office, pulled the blinds and thought about it. Then, it hit him to call a friend and the original detective on the case for a consult.

On the second ring, the line picked up. "Private Investigations, this is Detective Soprano, what can I do for you?"

"Soprano, this is Vasquez. I need you to get your butt down here first thing in the morning for a consult."

Soprano responded, "What is it this time, missing persons, string of burglaries, two crews about to go to war?"

Captain Vasquez was silent for a minute before he said, "No, it's about the Widow Maker. We may have him in custody. I want you in the viewing room with me watching interrogations."

It had been damn near four years since he had heard that name. A flood of nasty memories of encountering victims, their families, and the press all flooded his mind. Soprano sat up in bed in the corner of his shoebox studio apartment slash office and put his glasses on. He grabbed an old metallic brown file from his desktop labeled Carlos McIntyre and said, "I can come now. Give me twenty minutes and I will be right there."

Captain Vasquez said, "I have got a parking lot full of press that I have to address. There is a growing crowd of civilians with the potential to become a mob, I need to disperse. Plus, it will be good to let these suspects sweat for a couple hours."

Soprano cut in, "Suspects. How many are we talking about here?"

Captain Vasquez said, "Just get your butt down here around 5am. I will walk you through all of the details before we go to the observation room."

"I will be there, you can count on me Vasquez," Soprano replied.

Captain Vasquez said, "Good. I will see you tomorrow then and by the way Soprano, one of the detectives on this case is nothing like you and me. He's a hotshot rookie, not from out of our backyard. Still, he has been pulling in some big arrests. So, he may appear to come across a little sideways since he's gunning for your old job. None of that is on you. You're coming for my peace of mind and to hopefully put a nice bow on this case. Lastly, you might want to shave, because there may be some press here that may recognize you."

"Will do Vasquez, and thanks for the heads up. I will see you at 5am," said Soprano and then he hung up the phone. Soprano removed the rubber bands from the old folder and began to review the worst case of his career. A case that cost him the trust of the community, made a media spectacle out of the Brooklyn Park Police Department, and led to the stroke that drove him into retirement. While he carefully reviewed every note that he had written in that file and restudied the crime scene photos from each gruesome slaying, his eyes grew heavy. In his dream, he walked through Sever's labyrinth in Shakopee, Minnesota. For over twenty years, this elaborate maze structure just outside of Canterbury Park had been cut into a nine feet tall cornfield. It has served as a popular nighttime attraction that spans the month of October and in specific, the week of

Halloween. In the dream, Detective Soprano found himself walking down a long narrow path by himself. The sound of crawling locusts upon the leaves echoed throughout the field. The hunters moon sat low on the horizon and gave a fluorescent glow to the foot of hazy fog that covered the ground. He pinched the collar of his jacket closed that he used to block off the chill of the air that swept up and down the aisles. In his right hand was a brochure that contained a map to help lost individuals find their way out of the maze. When he opened it to study the map, he felt shocked to learn that it was blank. Huge, blood-soaked raindrops fell on the labyrinth as he noticed a dark figure dressed in white at the end of the path before him on a cross beam like a scarecrow. The Widow Maker raised his head and smiled at him from underneath the fedora style brim through a jawline partly covered with decayed flesh.

In fear, Detective Soprano reached for his gun and found that the holster was empty. As the Widow Maker dismounted the beam, Detective Soprano turned and fled. The Widow Maker pursued him part of the way down the narrow pathway, then disappeared into the cornfield. Weakened from advanced age, Soprano's slow run became an awkward wobble and he fell. Consumed by fear, he continuously watched over his shoulder while getting up. Finally, he stumbled half blind around a corner and into a dead end within the maze, he quickly tried to double back and found himself boxed in a 3 feet by 3 feet space. Slowly, the cornstalks rattled and swayed as someone etched their way through the fields towards him. Just before the last of the cornstalk barrier between them was breached, the figure on the other side stopped. Detective Soprano listened to the sound of deep breaths permeate the stalks until he heard a dry, disturbed voice ask, "Whom do you seek Detective?"

Soprano responded, "I know who you are Carlos, and I am coming for you."

The Widow Maker laughed sadistically and said, "Do not incite my wrath, you impotent parasite. The only reason why I have allowed you to remain is for mere sport. When I am done toying with you, I will swiftly hang you by the neck with your entrails and swing you from the mantel of your door."

Hearing the unseen image move closer to him through the cornfield, Detective Soprano felt the impended impact of those words. Wisely, he avoided a response to that statement and asked, "Why are you doing this Carlos?"

No answer came except the sound of the Widow Maker as he walked away back through the cornfield. Soprano shouted, "Not this time Carlos! You have tortured me for six years and dammit, I want answers!" Still, no response came. Only the sound of Animus as he moved further and further away. Detective Soprano swallowed slow and hard as he stepped in between the stalks and began to follow the Widow Maker. With each step that he took, the stalks began to close in tighter and tighter around him. Being compressed in the field, he struggled to move and tried to fight his way through it until the thicket of it all became so dense that he became suspended in mid step with one leg caught in the air and his arms were trying to dig through the vined stalks.

He yelled, "Carlos!" in the direction that he had thought he had travelled in. Then, suddenly a chill swept over his flesh as a cold hand reached through the stalks, grabbed his spine, and squeezed his soul. Behind him, he heard the Latin inscription of the Widow Maker, "Lux Ab Exitium Velle Venere" echo at the far end of the opposite side of the field.

Detective Soprano awoke sweating profusely in his bed. Papers from the file he had been reading were glued to his chest. A crime scene photo of the Skinny Pimp, his best source of information potentially leading to the whereabouts of Carlos McIntyre, was balled up in his hand. The decapitated slain pimp had been found sitting in a chair at the old Brick's grocery store with his head in his lap underneath the Latin inscription. He slowly released the photo from the death grip of his hand and wiped the thick sweat from his forehead.

"I am getting too old for this shit," he whispered to himself as he glanced at the clock on the wall above the empty stained coffee pot. He closed his eyes and mumbled, "Its 5:17 am."

Slowly, the realization dawned on him that he was supposed to already have been at the Brooklyn Park

Police Department by 5am. "Dammit, I am late again!" he yelled, "Vasquez is going to be pissed. Man, I need this consultation to boost my clientele for private investigations."

He quickly sat up and pulled on the same wrinkled dress pants that he had worn for the last three days. When he reached for his shoes, he heard a loud known on his apartment door, "Boom, Boom."

Confused as to who would be at his door at 5 in the morning, Soprano yelled, "Hang on!" and reached for his gun holster that hung on the headboard. Everyone in this drug infested neighborhood knew exactly who he was. Many still saw him as a cop and he was not about to take any chances because of that.

"Boom. Boom."

"I said hang on!" He shouted irritated. Then, he moved catlike until he was pressed firmly against the cool surface of the wall. He removed his firearm from its holster, rested his finger on the trigger, softly set the barrel against the door, and looked through the peek hole. His facial expression changed the moment he investigated the hall and saw the two uniformed officers talking to each other. One was holding a cup of coffee.

Soprano removed both door locks, opened the door, and said, "Let me guess. Captain Vasquez sent you?"

CHAPTER 21
WHO'S CRYING WOLF?

By the time Captain Vasquez and Detective Soprano stepped out of the observation room halfway through interrogations, HLN Morning Express with Robin Meade had already circulated the story of an arrest in the Widow Maker slaying several times across their national news desk. Maria sat at the kitchen table next to Jaysaiah in his highchair watching the report. As soon as Carlos came downstairs, she quickly turned the TV channel to an infomercial and acted as if she was talking to their son. Carlos knew her all too well. Especially how she loves to flip back and forth between two or three news channels in the morning. He instantly knew something was off when he heard her turn off the TV before he came around the corner. When he reached for the remote to the TV, she quickly tried to distract him and asked, "Hey, what do you want to do today? I was thinking that we could possibly drive down toward the cities and meet your mom somewhere?"

Carlos eyed her curiously and said, "I don't know if today will work. It may be better for me to call and get my mom's schedule at work. Then, have a currier deliver her a message by hand to her job for precautionary reasons."

Next, Maria acted as if she was trying to find something in a cabinet by the TV to block the picture. Carlos gently pushed her aside, moved a chair directly up on the screen, turned the channel back, and tried to listen. The more he tried to listen, the more Maria tried to talk above the top stories of the day. It had been no more than seven to ten minutes into the broadcast that pictures of Ra'zee and Mei Wei came up on the screen above the title "Two Suspects Arrested in the Twin Cities Widow Maker Killings."

When Carlos saw the headline, he zeroed in on the photos to get a good look at the police mugshots. Maria went silent as he turned up the volume on the TV sky high. After he heard the brief report about the string of robberies, burglaries, and homicides attached to the Widow Maker's name within the last year, at a commercial break he quietly stood up as a look of deep malice and boiling contempt grew on his face. He turned off the TV, dropped his head momentarily in contemplation then left the kitchen in haste. Maria didn't know what to think as she sat there and listened to the sound of him climb the steps one by one until the soft latch of the attic door opened and then clicked shut.

Carlos went and sat cross legged on the floor in front of the barren brick wall that had opened before to the domain of the Widow Maker. Slowly, he began his chant of the Latin inscription, "Lux Ab Exitium Velle Venere." Below the chant, the sound of playful chatter from the girls, Rita and Katherine, could be heard downstairs.

Maria, who went to lay their son down for a nap, yelled from the kitchen, "Stop all of that jumping in this house before you wake up your brother Jaysiah." Then, the soft cries of a baby filled the air over running bath water.

Within a few short minutes of repeating the Latin mantra, the brick mortar lines on the wall in front of him cracked and a door to a very dark place opened. The sound of bone being crushed underneath the sheer weight of someone's' footsteps filled his hearing until the Light of Death Himself ascended from within the cavernous hallway. When the Widow Maker came and stood over him, Carlos thought it was rather off that he did not hear the familiar chime of six nickels falling to the ground, nor did his vision grow hazy. Those were signs that typically served as a herald or a precursor to the impending present of the Widow Maker. Also, he did not feel the usual student to teacher vibe about this encounter, but rather a client to contract killer. The Widow Maker looked at Carlos, then past him as if through the looking glass of time to another version of himself. It was then that Carlos remembered the day that he was taken past, present, and future across their legacy, and to remind him of the importance of their work.

Carlos asked, "Am I here?"

The Widow Maker responded chillingly, "Why have you summoned me yet again, our work is complete."

Carlos stared at the floor and said, "While you slumber, our work is in danger. Someone is making a mockery of our work. They have stolen from us by using our legacy for thievery."

The Widow Maker's eyes turned an insidious yellow as he yelled, "What?!"

Carlos continued, "We must return. Make them pay. Make them all remember our name."

Slowly, the Widow Maker tilted his head back. An intense stretch tightened across his body as he slowly rolled his shoulders and cracked his neck. His eyes rolled into the back of his partially flesh covered head as he responded with bite and vengeance in his voice. Through his teeth, he hissed, "Follow me, our work begins again now."

He turned back into the cavernous hallway and Carlos slowly arose and followed him through the veil into the obscure darkness.

Back in the hall outside of the observation and

interrogation rooms, a Sergeant from the Brooklyn Park PD, a detective in Wisconsin, and a lawyer from the Public Defender's Office who was representing Ra'zee and Mei Wei, walked off. Detective Soprano told Captain Vasquez, "This is a waste of time. These two may be guilty of murdering Leonard Johns and committing a laundry list of other crimes, but they are not the Widow Maker."

Captain Vasquez looked disappointed at him as he shook his head. Then, he said, "Now why doesn't that surprise me? So, give me one reason why is it that you are so sure that these two are not the Widow Maker?"

Detective Soprano smiled and said, "I will do better than that. I will give you four. Number one: The Widow Maker never places the initials of his tag name by the victim. Number two: except for Richard Thompson, aka Skinny Pimp, where the murder wasn't business as usual, but highly personal, he had always placed six nickels in the eyes of his victims as a fee for the Boatman. Third: the only message he writes above a victim is a Latin inscription of "Lux Ab Exitium Velle Venere" which translates as Light of Death Will Come."

Soprano walked over to get some water from the bubbler. Vasquez asked, "Okay, but what's the fourth thing?"

Soprano whispered to himself through light shivers as the ice-cold water filtered through his system. "Damn, that's good water. I really need to start drinking more water."

After two more cups, he walked back over to Vasquez as he repeated, "the fourth thing?"

Soprano asked, "what?"

Vasquez repeated, "The fourth reason you were about to tell me as to why those two in there are not the Widow Maker?"

Soprano said, "Oh yeah, the Widow Maker is a methodical killer whose primary killing tools are a scalpel and a hypodermic needle. He believes he's teaching penance to those that fall on his list while deterring others from the same or similar acts. He's not a petty thief. If he takes anything from a victim, it will be a bone fragment from their body as a trophy. Whether it be vertebrae, fingers, toes, etc. This may be a way he relives each slaughter?"

As Matthews walked into the hall, Soprano smiled at him as he walked over and continued, "My guess is these two stole the tag name in order to mask their first homicide, and later turned it into profit. Which was probably Decimal's hair brain scheme."

Matthews snapped, "You're old and washed up. The reason you never caught the Widow Maker and had so much trouble with identity is because all along, it was this husband-and-wife copycat team. A man and a woman, not this kid you thought it was and never proved. Now watch and learn as I clean up the mess you left after you let the Widow Maker duo get away in the first place."

Soprano tried to plead with him, "First, you've got

your wires crossed. These two are killers but not the Widow Maker. Second, watch how you talk to me, son. Don't let your alligator mouth get you into something your hummingbird ass can't get you out of!"

While they argued, a uniformed cop came around the corner and shouted, "Excuse me Captain Vasquez, Sergeant has requested you in the break room up front right away. Trust me, you will want to see this."

Vasquez responded, "Damit, what is it now?"

A KARE 11 breaking news report detailed a horrific scene on how last night, a trail of bodies was found in Rochester appearing to be the handiwork of the Widow Maker. Captain Vasquez listened to the account and the physical description of the victims. The main murder instruments were a scalpel and hypodermic needle. Each of the victims had six nickels in replacement of their missing eyes. While still watching the report, Vasquez told the Seargeant, "Call and see if you can get Rochester's Chief of Police on the phone for me?"

Then he shouted in the hall, "Matthews, get your butt in here."

Matthews stuck his head around the corner and asked, "What's up Cap?"

Vasquez didn't even look at him as he said, "Cut those two suspects loose."

Matthews protested, "But Cap?"

Vasquez shouted, "Now Matthews! Then meet in my office."

Matthews looked at Detective Soprano who threw his

hands up and smiled. No sooner than the two stepped out of the break room that the front door to the station opened and closed. A lady in the lobby, who came to pay off a parking ticket before work, screamed. The sound of multiple boots and shouts from the Sergeant to lock it down filled the air. Vasquez and Soprano ran toward the lobby and was met by a gruesome scene. A drunken abusive father, that has sent his pregnant wife to the hospital nine times over six pregnancies with a broken jaw, lacerated forehead, cigarette burns, and multiple belt buckle bruises, stumbled in the police station. He was naked, beaten, and had frost bitten feet. A small incision severed his vocal cords so that he couldn't speak. His only clothing was a placard made of rotten wood hanging from a hemp rode. Carved into his chest by a surgical instrument in dry blood read the Latin inscription, "Lux Ab Exitium Velle Venere". He wreaked of feces and standing there blind from the six nickels that replaced his eyes urinated on himself which caused a female officer to vomit. While one officer moved to wrap him in a blanket, Decimal and Jade were brought up front from the interrogation room for release. Jade paused when she saw the disfigured man in the lobby. Although his eyes read fear, Decimal had an image to protect so he didn't flinch.

Detective Soprano yelled at them from across the room, "You two idiots have no idea what you have brought on yourself. The Widow Maker will come for you."

Decimal replied, "I am sick and tired of your scare tactics. The more you talk, the more all of this reminds me of the little boy who cried wolf."

Detective Soprano replied, "You do know how that story ends right? With a real damn wolf!"

Vasquez yelled at Matthews, "Get them the hell out of here and clear this damn lobby for the paramedics. Let's get a perimeter check done to make sure that there aren't any more half naked victims out in the parking lot that need medical attention."

Soprano walked over the window and mumbled to himself, "I am getting too old for this shit. Carlos, I am ready for you this time. So, let's finish this once and for all." He turned to Vasquez and said, "Hey Cap, I have got a lead to follow up on. I will be in touch."

Vasquez said, "Now is not the time to pull a lone ranger Soprano. I need all hands-on deck."

Soprano replied, "Sure thing Cap. I just figured with the return of the Widow Maker that Carlos McIntyre is bound to show up at his mother's house. You won't find him. So, I am going to wait for him. I will keep you posted." He turned then walked out past the medics coming in the door.

Vasquez yelled, "Don't do anything without my approval. This is still official police business."

Soprano mumbled, "Tell that to Carlos McIntyre."

Later that day after their release, when Ra'zee and Mei Wei got home, she decided to go out for a drink to unwind. Carlos, having already done thorough research on both of them, followed her from their home to the Stargate Nightclub. The club was basically empty except for a few security officers and management staff hanging out. Jade looked pathetic as she nursed the Taka Vodka pint bottle that she had smuggled into the club from the Ten O' Clock liquor store.

CHAPTER 22
BELLY OF THE FISH

———◦c◦◦c◦———

Carlos watched as people avoided going over next to Jade to reorder their drinks at the bar. After, she finished the last of her drink and slammed the empty bottle on the countertop. Upset at the fact she had no money for a drink and couldn't open a tab because she hadn't paid her last bill and no one wanted her there because every time she drank there, it ended up being some bullshit in the club. She stood to leave and bumped into Carlos, who was holding a fist full of cash with a million-dollar smile.

Carlos shot his best Mack look at her and said, "Leaving so soon? I was hoping to indulge you to celebrate my rebirth with me, I mean, my birthday with me."

Jade smiled and said, "Sure, I was about to leave

because I had no one to keep me company."

Truth of the matter was that standing there, she looked like the mangy alley cat that you would shoo away from your house. The skintight dark purple t-shirt dress she was wearing was half clean with what looked like dried semen on the hemline right between her legs. Her eye shadow and foundation makeup application were way too thick. Her lips were dry and cracked in several places, like the heels of her feet. The bottoms of her feet were soiled like muck on the floor of a silo caked with a decayed vegetable matter. Delusional, she believed that she was highly attractive and irresistible to all men in a respectable manner.

Carlos tried to drown her in vodka, but soon discovered that she had the tolerance of a goat and drank like bottom feeding catfish. Two hours drifted by in the blink of an eye and more patrons started to stroll in. To further seclude her, he suggested that they shoot darts over in the corner. It was there that he emptied the contents of two capsules of Valium into her drinks. When the powerful sedative took hold of her, her speech slurred, and she could barely walk. Carlos placed her arm over his shoulder and proceeded to take her outside to the parking lot, past security. Having seen her a drunken mess several times before, they thought nothing of it even when she tried to signal to someone for help while he loaded her into the back of his stolen car., once she was in the backseat of the car, Carlos began to hear the familiar chimes of six nickels falling to the ground as his vision grew hazy.

The Widow Maker placed a chloroform-soaked handkerchief over her mouth to render her unconscious. When Mei Wei awoke, she had been stripped naked, dressed in sackcloth, and chained to the floor of a condemned butcher storage room inside an abandoned warehouse not too far from Hope Harbor. She stumbled to her feet and tried to inch her way towards a faint light that streaked underneath the heavy steel sliding door. A medieval contraption of fetters made from rusted twined barbwire pierced her ankles and wrists, causing her to scream in pain behind every step she took. A short chain connecting the dog collar on her neck with the restraint belt around her waist caused her to walk hunched over. She felt highly disoriented behind the effects of the Valium and the chloroform that disrupted her natural senses. The lingering smell of rotten meat, dead mice, and bile filled the cooler.

Through snot filled sobs, she began to cry, "Help! Is anybody there? Somebody please help me. Ra'zee!"

On the other side of the door, the Widow Maker, dressed in all white, stood looking out across the abandoned industrial park. Slowly, he seethed through his teeth, "Ananias, let's see where your heart truly lies. Is it for the love of money, or for Sapphire thy wife?"

When he pulled open the heavy sliding door, natural light from the setting sun blinded Jade. Instantly, her petition for mercy spilled forth. With her hand blocking the disorienting light, she couldn't make out the face of

Carlos, who stood in the doorway. "Please don't hurt me. You must have me confused with someone else, but you can still let me go. If its money you want, my husband will pay you. Please, just let me call him."

Cold and unaffectionate, the Widow Maker told her, "Why, Mrs. Lajoune, I had hoped for more. If you really want to be released, you should make your performance more theatrical like drooling begging, or uncontrollable sobbing and shivering. I know maybe vomit or defecating on yourself would score you high points." He looked contemplative at the floor and then added, "My, my. I haven't seen that one in a while."

Mei Wei responded in confusion, "What?"

The Widow Maker laughed and said, "Let me be clear Jade, I cannot be bargained with. I have no sentiment for pity for remorse."

She yelled back at him, "You sick freak, let me the hell out of here!"

The Widow Maker smiled and said, "There you are. I knew you were hiding in there. Like Jonah in the belly of the fish. If you think about it, you should be thanking me. For it was in the belly of the great fish that Jonah realized his true calling. However, in this story you shall be my Jonah as I chastise you like God and send you forth as my messenger to the unrepentant. That all may remember my name and know that it is unwise to transgress against the Widow Maker."

Jade screamed, "No! Wait, I am sorry, I didn't know!" as he slammed the heavy cooler door shut, plunging her back into darkness. On the other side of the door as he put a heavy padlock on the door, he whispered to her, "Welcome to the belly of the fish."

Jade continued to beg as she listened to the sound of his footsteps slowly walk away. Over the next three days, at precisely 3:00 am, Carlos used Mei Wei's cellphone to send Ra'zee several Instagram video clips of her being tortured. The first day showed her being water boarded with vodka for a detailed confession in stealing the Widow Maker's name. The second day showed her fear-filled eyes as her mind crack from reality while he took flashbulb pictures of her from several different spots inside the dark storage room. The third day showed her being hogtied and hoisted up by a chain across a steel beam in the center of the floor. Next, the Widow Maker placed a large rat inside a bag and tied it over her head. Violently, she screamed as the bag shook. Minutes later, the screams stopped, but the bag continued to rattle. A high-pitched screech of the rat rang out, then the soft snap of bone could be heard from inside the bag. When he removed the bag, Mei Wei had several scratches on her face, a wild look in her eyes, and half of the body of the dead rat hanging out of her mouth. Then, the picture shifted to the ground as she urinated on herself.

Ra'zee grimaced as the Widow Maker took a pair of metal shears and cut off her ring fingers and toes one by one. That same night, he sent the severed finger and toes of Mei Wei to Ra'zee by mail currier in a small white gift box with the address to the building. Attached was a note that read, "Be here within the next thirty minutes alone or I will kill her. If you are late, I will send you more little white boxes as a reminder. First ten minutes, a hand. Twenty minutes, a foot. So, you'd better hurry, because your wife is literally falling to pieces."

Ra'zee wasted no time in heading over there to get Mei Wei. When he arrived, the Widow Maker lured him upstairs to her through a scattered trail of her belongings. First, there was one of her sandals used to prop open the side entrance door. Inside, he followed the sound of her screaming and pleading on a recording of her being tortured. In the corner of the room, the light on Mei Wei's cellphone glowed brightly. Sitting on top of it was her wedding ring. Beneath it, the recorded video feed of her being tortured ran in a loop. While he lifted the phone and looked at the blood on her wedding band, the Widow Maker covered her face with a cloth and poured a half of a gallon of hydrochloric acid over her mouth. As Mei Wei choked violently behind the solvent, the Widow Maker tilted his head back and inhaled the sweet, rotten egg like scent produced by the lungs as if it were a rare wine, a chosen relic to be savored in a cup.

Ra'zee shook his head in deep regret. Flashbacks of the geeky looking girl that he had fallen in love with inside a record shop flooded his mind. Beautiful memories of her standing in the rain in mixed-matched orange slice and kiwi green colored ankle socks soaking wet sheltered in his arms on the night she was cut off from her family. He stopped the video and put her ring into his pocket. Faintly through the streetlight outside, he noticed a shadow cross the floor at the top of the stairs.

Ra'zee yelled, "Mei Wei! Beautiful, are you up there?"

After the echo of his voice trailed off, in silence he heard a slight rattle of a chain. Quickly, he climbed the stairs and found Mei Wei hogtied and hoisted up in the middle of the floor by a heavy chain. She smelled horrible. Streaks of bile had dried on her inner thighs. Urine ran down her legs and dripped into a small puddle on the floor beneath her. Thinking that she was dead, he slowly kissed her on the forehead and cried. Sobs and confessions of how much he loved her whispered across the floor. Suddenly, Mei Wei coughed and sharply inhaled as she struggled through a chemically scorched throat to speak.

Ra'zee quickly said, "Beautiful! I am so glad I found you. Don't worry, I am going to get you out of here."

She continued to struggle through dry whispers to warn him while he looked around in paranoia, so he asked, "What is it?"

When he placed his right ear next to her lips, a faint whisper came through slow stutters, "Hh-e's st-st-ill h-he-re."

Out of a dark corner, Ra'zee heard a voice say, "I see you discovered my trail of breadcrumbs."

Then, out walked the Widow Maker dressed in all white. Several large black crows flew in front of him.

When Ra'zee saw him, he immediately charged in his direction. He only got about four or five feet before he tripped the military grade razor wire that snapped and severed both of his feet from his legs above his ankles. The Widow Maker uttered loudly, "Lux Ab Exitium Velle Venere" as his eyes broke the plane of darkness and his pupils split in two, revealing a smaller set of pupils in the upper corner of his eyes.

Decimal screamed in horrendous pain as Carlos came and stood over him. A primal shiver swept over his flesh as he cracked his neck and said, "Still don't believe in the Widow Maker Decimal?"

Mei Wei dryly asked, "Ra'zee, babe, are you okay?"

Ra'zee pleaded through short breaths as panic took hold of him, "Wait, this is all of my fault. Please just take me and let her go!"

The Widow Maker responded coldly as he moved swiftly over to the center beam and lifted up his home-made version of the Roman cat-o-nine tails secured to it "When you pray for the rain, you have to deal with the mud. I cannot be bargained with. I feel no pity or remorse. There will only be salvation through the light of death. That all may know and respect my name. I am Animus. Egyptian Blackness, The Light of Death Himself, the Widow Maker. Now, hold your tongue for your soul has a date with the Boatman."

With heavy, violet thrusts, the scourge fell and shredded Ra'zee's back until his flesh lay completely open to the bone. Mei Wei's last thoughts fell on the words of her mother, who had warned her about true darkness that was coming for her.

Outside, on the sidewalk, the rattle of shopping cartwheels could be heard beneath the window as old lady Sheila Parker made her final trip back to Hope Harbor. She paused briefly and looked up to the hunched silhouette of the Widow Maker on the wall as he scourged Ra'zee. Quietly, she whispered to herself, "Maybe now, we can both rest?" Then, slowly she pushed her shopping cart on toward her cardboard shelter behind the Greyhound bus station.

The following morning as Ra'zee and Mei Wei's bodies were being discovered by an anonymous tip, Detective Soprano sat in his car half of a block from Carmen McIntyre's house. He watched as the small family dressed as if they were headed to church was greeted on the front porch. There was a serene look on the face of Carlos when his mom kissed him on the forehead. Lovingly, she stooped down and hugged her granddaughters Rita and Katherine. Her heart melted when she lifted the toddler from his mother's arms.

Maria smiled as McIntyre cried lightly and kissed the chubby cheeks of her only grandson Jaysiah. Quickly, she shuttled them inside as she looked protectively up and down the quiet street to see if they had been followed and to ensure that they were safe. Detective Soprano could tell that something had changed. That whatever darkness that had once had a grip on this family was gone. Instinctively, he reached for his cellphone to call it in to Captain Vasquez. While the phone rang in Vasquez's office, Soprano thought about all that he had endured over the last six years of his life. He was tired of it all and wanted out too. Just before Vasquez answered the phone, thoughts about the warning the Widow Maker gave him, when he dreamed about the labyrinth, crossed his mind.

"I am getting too old for this shit," he whispered to himself.

Vasquez picked up and immediately asked, "Soprano, what do you got?"

Soprano responded emptily, "The mother's house was a dead end. The kid never showed."

Vasquez replied, "Dammit! I was hoping a new lead would have turned up."

Soprano dryly said, "Sorry Cap, maybe next time."

Vasquez said, "Keep me posted and let me know if you come up with any ides. I don't want this guy to getaway again."

Soprano said, "I hear you Cap, neither do I, but maybe that's how this story ends."

Vasquez had known Soprano for over twenty-five years. In that time, he had never known him to give up on a suspect, especially not one as heinous as the Widow Maker. So whatever darkness he had experienced, the price of a piece of his soul was enough payment for that. Vasquez knew what that was personally like from the days when he investigated the Golden State Killer.

He simply said, "Goodbye Soprano, you are a fine

detective and it's been a privilege working with you. Take care of yourself and call if you need anything."

"Will do Cap, and thanks for everything," replied Soprano as they both hung up.

EPILOGUE:
DELIVERANCE

S heila Parker lay still with a malaria-like fever under shallow breaths. The rest of the homeless camp was out busy pan – handling and picking through garbage cans throughout the Twin Cities. Their hopes were to find something of value that they could either trade or sell for money. Suddenly, she heard the sound of several sets of footsteps approach the doorway of her cardboard shelter. The shadow of a large hand scratched at the plastic blue tarp until it found its opening and pulled it aside. In came the hand of a man who handed her six nickels as a fee for the Boatman. A token of well done and release after being the faithful griot of the Widow Maker for over half of a decade. The small family stood there momentarily in honorable silence, then walked off. The playful chatter of two little girls and a boy could be heard in the backdrop as their little dress shoes skipped across the gravel.

Hours later, on the shores of the netherworld, the Boatman drew close to dock and as usual Skinny Pimp, who had been stranded there for three years now because he had no fee for the Boatman, approached him and tried to negotiate with those on board. Old lady Sheila Parker, the only soul on the boat that still had both of her eyes, looked and saw her old friend Skinny Pimp. She could tell that he had grown humbled and was broken. Moved with compassion, she decided to sacrifice herself and gave her coins to him.

The raspy old voice said, "Here, this is for you. The time has come for you to move on to purgatory. I will take your place here for a while. You go on towards forgiveness."

Startled by the act of grace, he mumbled a thousand praises of thanksgiving as he quickly felt for the edge of the boat and gave the fee to the Boatman. Although he couldn't see it, old lady Sheila Parker waved to him from the shore. Hours later, when nothing else could be heard on the boat except the splash of the oars in the water and the chains on deck, it dawned on him why the voice of his salvation, although aged, sounded so familiar. He scurried to his feet and with all of his might, shouted her name over and over again until it echoed across the sky.

"Va-ni-ty! Sh-el-I-a! Thank you. I'll never forget you."

On the shore, an angelic smile graced old lady Parker's face as her sacrifice transformed her into dazzling light and propelled her across the abyss, like the others who did not need the boat ride.

ABOUT THE AUTHOR

Zoez Lajoune was born in Wauwatosa, Wisconsin. He studied creative writing at the college of St. Scholastica in Duluth, Minnesota, under Dr. Zelman. He now lives in Coleraine, Minnesota. Watch for Book 4 of the Widow Maker Series: The God Complex. Coming soon.

PREVIEW OF THE WIDOW MAKER
BOOK 4: THE GOD COMPLEX

———————⊸∘⊂◠⊃∘⊸———————

While Dr. Rutkowski gave a dark lecture to six of the nine remaining patients at the asylum. One patient was out ill, another one in physical therapy, and the last one in isolation for disruptive behavior. Nevaeh Sharai stood quietly in the corner of the small study next to a bookshelf and listened. All the patients knew the real reason Raquel was now three days in the quiet room. She had spoken strongly against Dr. Rutowski in group and committed the cardinal sin by telling a local interviewing college student about the real asylum. While Dr. Rutowski stood in front of the small group, Nevaeh fingered through fresh pages of horrors in her mind like topical index cards in a drawer at a library. She recalled the look upon the faces of a misfit group of touring students as they entered the maze of the asylum. They did not belong there, but he had chosen them all.

Dry dead leaves blew in from outside as the group stumbled through the two heavy front doors into the empty lobby. She arose from her desk to intercept, but a hand on her shoulder from Dr. Rutowski made her sit. Each of them had a black envelope in their hand formally sealed with a red piece of wax that bore the initials TWM, the invitation of the Widow Maker into the belly of the beast. Everyone turned and looked behind them when the sound of the heavy doors echoed as they closed and locked them all inside. One frightened girl jumped and dropped her pad of paper for notes and folder in her arms. Suddenly, a warm, hospitable, eloquent and relaxing voice spoke, "Good morning. I am Dr. Marcus Rutowski. Welcome to Stonewall Asylum. If my memory serves me correctly, you are Karen," he said as he pointed to the tall slender, dorky-looking blonde whose skin was as pale as the backside of an Irish man's kneecaps. She nodded in agreement. He smiled and said, "Excellent." Then he turned his gaze on yet another student. "Alexander?" he asked while nodding to a chubby looking lad who dabbed at a jelly donut stain on his sleeveless sweatshirt just below his bowtie. He in return nodded while he said, "Doctor."

"You are the easiest selection to remember Calvin," Dr. Rutowski said to the only black guy in the group who fumbled through an old satchel. He spoke very rapidly, "Thank you very much for this opportunity, Dr. Rutowski. I took the liberty of bringing you a copy of my resume. Might I add your last lecture on dual diagnostic therapy was brilliant. Especially the part about," Dr. Rutowski raised a hand and said, "Please Calvin, later. There will be plenty of time to discuss the myriad of lectures I've given over the years."

A student in the group mumbled under her breath, though her words still carried volume in the empty hall, "Brown nose." Dr. Rutowski quickly said, "That would make you Camille." He said to the anorexic white girl in Gothic style clothing. Her outfit consisted of black turtleneck skintight T-shirt, heavy blue jean jacket, dark blue skirt, and combat boots with spiked wristbands. She had on thick black eyeliner and dark purple lipstick with short choppy hair. All she said in response was, "Bingo," while she turned her head, rolled her eyes, and popped her chewing gum. Dr. Rutowski commented, "Interesting, very interesting." He turned his gaze yet again to Terrance, a transgender student undergoing hormone injections as part of his final preparation to change fully into a woman from being a man. Before Dr. Rutowski could speak, a peppered voice said, "Everyone knows me, I'm Terri." However, the smile quickly left behind Dr. Rutowski's gender opinionated response of, "Welcome Terrance." He nodded to the last individual and said, "It's a pleasure to see you again Ethan." Ethan was a four feet nine-inch-tall sophomore and recent intern there, who looked as though he had been born and bred in a lab. Slowly turning to leave he said, "All of you please follow me." A bitter demanding response firmly spoke up from the back of the group, "It's Teri!"

Dr. Rutowski began to hear the familiar chime of six nickels falling to the ground as his vision grew hazy. A soul drinking stare underscored by an angelic smile turned and fell upon Teri as the Widow Maker said, "Really. We'll have to work on that now, won't we?" Teri looked at the floor. Calvin the eager one interjected, "Some of us are very excited about rumors of a new internship program starting here at the asylum. That is said to replace several staff positions." The Dark One responded, "All of you are on my list." Like lost children they ventured further inside the lair like Hansel and Gretel by the Witch's candy to the oven. Not knowing that there was no way that the Widow Maker would ever allow either of them to leave the asylum.

The further they ventured down the hall of this elaborate maze, the more several of the students noticed the skeleton crew of staff members that abode at the asylum. When they entered the main group room Raquel rushed over to Ethan and grabbed his hand. Her eyes wide with eagerness. Her hands clammy and cold. She began to tell him about the strange occurrences that as of late had become the new norm there. Ethan almost vomited at the smell of Raquel's breath and was terrified to death by her presence. Dr. Rutowski studied him carefully, curiously while Raquel gestured frantically to him with her hands.

After several moments he sought to swiftly end this encounter. Wisely, he motioned to the group, "For those of you who are truly invested in psychiatric care beyond the mere interactions of some of our more challenged individuals there are some basic protocols that we must always follow. This is for our own safety as well as the safety of the patients in our care. Patients who may periodically feel hostile when someone invades their personal space. Why in the serialized work of a sociopath like Raquel. She could easily slit your throat with a sharp chicken bone if you got too close and you'd never see it coming, right Ethan?" Ethan quickly stepped away from Raquel and said, "Correct Dr. Rutowski, four feet at all times." The other patients watched and huddled away from the tour group as if they were all carriers of some infectious airborne disease.

Most people believe that hindsight is 20/20 vision, that when most look back, they can clearly see the moves of a chess game play out up till the inevitable checkmate. Their eyes narrow at the bait to trap. The most coveted power piece on the board, the queen. Once the queen is taken by the allure of the pawn, most opponents defense collapse. The most prolific problem that Nevaeh saw when her mind drifted back to the game between her and Dr. Rutowski was her own passivity. She had stood idly by and did nothing to defend anyone from the psychosis of the Widow Maker. Her mind cringed as her extraordinary ability to recall highly vivid details kicked in. A collage of agonized patient faces lost in a world of mental cruelty swirled before her mind's eye. Patients that in her denial of the true mental state of Dr. Rutowski she had sent to their deathbeds. Her heart pounded terribly as she recalled how just a few nights ago she was almost one of those patients.

"This is ridiculous," Nevaeh said to herself as she walked over to the window, "What would any sane person do under these circumstances? Run! No one would blame my decision in the face of self-preservation. Yes, I should leave immediately, or perhaps in the middle of the night while most of the patients are asleep. I could leave around the time when Dr. Rutowski disappears after heading to his office. That would give me a good head start, but how will I get the main gate open?" As a security precaution the gate could only be electronically opened by two separate keypads operated at the same time. One keypad was in the front lobby at the security guard's desk. The other keypad was in the guard booth next to the main gate. A booth that since the decline in staff members Dr. Rutowski always kept the keys to on his person. If somehow, she was able to get the keys or override the system with an unanswered emergency response call, who would operate the inside keypad? This meant be willing to sacrifice themselves and stay behind so that the others could escape and survive? Speaking of surviving, there were only six patients that she actually knew where they were. The six that were right in front of her. Dr. Rutowski claimed that he had discharged the other patients long ago. She had believed this too, until she found that patient's file in his room. A file she was certain that something in him wanted to kill her for. Why were the contents of that file so important? Was he trying to hide the fact that she had never left the asylum? What if none of them had left? What if they were still there or worse? There was something about the gleam in Dr. Rutowski's eyes as he spoke to her. His look told her that there were more survivors, but where? Where did he constantly disappear to? At times it was as if he vanished into thin air or simply walked through the walls. Then a horrifying thought crossed her mind. Could he be connected to the screams that permeated through the floors at night? Screams that were like the early morning dew upon the grass. Slowly it appeared and covered everything. Thick screams that saturated the soil of their minds and plowed the fields of fear in their hearts.

Nevaeh knew that the terror in the eyes of the patients at the asylum was due to the dark side of Dr. Rutowski. The warning bells going off in her mind were drowned out as Dr. Rutowski's muffled voice returned to her ears. His words were like the Dark Spider that spins a web ten times stronger than Kevlar and can easily bind human prey. At times when he spoke, he used dual hidden phrases to someone about them. They initially perceived it was about someone else. Later he repeated the phrase so they would finally make the connection.

Most disturbingly he told the group one day, "The secret to an exceptional rose is not the six to eight hours of sunlight and a wide place to spread its roots as some think. No, its cradle and fragility of life is found in warm blood and quiet darkness. The rose craves what is in the human veins. All the nitrates it desires is in that red gold. . . flowing within your arms. The rose of life craves such therapy." As well such language reminded her daily that she was trapped.

She watched as the Widow Maker performed many cruel torturous acts with fiery vengeance upon those that came across his path by false pretenses so that they could evade the judgement of mankind. She recalled how he plotted and abducted Calvin. Halfway through the tour he lured him to his office to allegedly discuss hiring him. Nevaeh thought it was very strange when he came back alone. Moments later when Karen asked where he was at, the Widow Maker told her that, "although Calvin had interned here before he regretted that he had an appointment that was necessary for him to attend. Still, he apologized for not completing the tour when I asked him to participate in it purely for moral support."

Meanwhile, Calvin sat bound in the basement chamber for moral judgement. The accusation against him was his attempt to start a rebellion and lead a coop to oust the good doctor from his authority. He had been sedated with an injection of hydrochlorothiazide in Dr. Rutowski's office. A shot that can reduce the heart rate so low a person will appear to have flat-lined. There was a small rubber meditation ball in his mouth, secured tightly by a long strip of gray duct tape wrapped about his head. He sat slumped over, unconscious in what the Widow Maker came to call the judgement seat. A medieval sitting post that looked like a cross between a baby's highchair and an old 1920s electric chair. It was made of a dark lime slick faggot wood. It had thick leather wrist straps on the arm posts of the chair. A small bell attached to a long hemp rope string rested on the earthen floor next to one of the front legs of the chair. By the other front leg was an old glass jar filled with what looked like huge leeches swimming in dirty sewage water. The Widow Maker tilted his chair backwards and water-boarded him with the dirty sewage-like water. He intentionally used a cloth with small holes in it so that the leeches could slither through. As he forcefully ingested the leeches they latched onto his trachea, esophagus, and diaphragm. Slowly they ate away at his internal tissue until he rapidly vomited through is nose and mouth while he defecated on himself.